Seven

A CLUB ALIAS NOVEL

KD Robichaux

Seven Production Crew

Editing by Hot Tree Editing
www.hottreeediting.com

Cover Design and
Formatting by Pink Ink Designs
www.pinkinkdesigns.com

Cover Photography by Justin James Cadwell
Edited by FuriousFotog
www.onefuriousfotog.com

Also by KD Robichaux

THE BLOGGER DIARIES TRILOGY
Wished for You
Wish He Was You
Wish Come True

No Trespassing

CONFESSION DUET
Before the Lie
Truth Revealed

CONFESSION DUET SPINOFF STANDALONES
(Can be read without the duet)
Seven: A Club Alias Novel

Coming Soon
Doc: A Club Alias Novel
Knight: A Club Alias Novel

Seven

Seven

Prologue

Twyla

I'm here.

I send the text, and then glance up over my steering wheel and through my windshield. It's pitch-black outside except for porch lights on at neighboring houses. My sister, Astrid, is in the one directly in front of me. The one-story house looks nice on the outside, painted a perfect, crisp white. The black shutters around the three windows and the red door give just enough pop to make the home look inviting. It's the perfect appearance to disguise the violence that goes on inside its walls.

I peek up into my rearview mirror. Paranoia mixes with my anxiety, raising my blood pressure enough I can feel my heart beat in my eardrums. I pray I don't see headlights come up behind me. The hell we would pay if we got caught....

"Come on, come on, sis," I whisper, squeezing the cell in my palm. My other hand fists around the steering wheel, nails digging in and knuckles turning white.

My tension rises until finally, I see the door straight ahead open and a shadow slips out of the house before it shuts again. My shoulders sag as a huge weight is lifted from them and I drop my phone between my thighs. As my sister's small frame crosses the street, I reach beneath my dash to pop the trunk for her.

She scurries to the back of my car and tosses in her bags before slamming it shut. I hit the unlock button just as she reaches for the handle, and the lights turn on as she yanks open the door. The sense of relief as I see her flushed face when she slips into the passenger seat makes me almost dizzy.

Until I spot the dark purple bruise around her left eye before she pulls the door closed behind her.

As the car goes black again, she presses a kiss to my cheek. My heart breaks a little, but then she whispers, "Thanks, Twy. Now drive. Brandon will be home soon."

That's all it takes. I shove my shifter into gear and speed out of the neighborhood.

And we don't look back for 2,673 miles.

One

Twyla

Two months later

"**YOUR WORK HISTORY IS FLAWLESS.** Your letter of recommendation from your previous employer is very impressive," Roxanne, the store manager says, looking down through her tiny-lensed readers at my application before glancing up at me over the rims. "But, darlin', you have a bachelors in chemical engineering. Why in the world do you want to work in my little shop? You're completely overqualified."

My shoulders slump. But at least she's asking me this now, instead of telling me in an e-mail denying me employment, like the other sixteen interviews I've been to in the past seven weeks.

"With all due respect, at this point, I will take anything I can get," I answer honestly.

She pulls off her glasses, folding her arms on top of her desk.

The middle-aged woman has an almost motherly air about her. Her frizzy blonde hair is pulled back into a ponytail away from her face. She would have been gorgeous in her prime. Her voice is kind. "Surely there is something better fitting for you, honey. I can only imagine the amount of work you had to put in to get that kind of degree. There must be—"

I can't hold it in any longer. And for the first time since we left California, I spill everything that's been circling inside my head, unable to confide in anyone. "My sister and I moved here for a fresh start. Halfway across the US, we googled a map of the country, closed our eyes, and where her finger landed, that's where we were going. I'm always the planner. When I was young, I would make an itinerary for every minute of our family vacations. To this day, I literally pencil in time to eat and sleep. She made me promise that this time, there would be no planning. No scheduling. We would leave it all up to fate. And this is where fate put us. Little did we know we would be planting ourselves in a small town outside a military base with nothing around but a shopping mall, tattoo shops, restaurants, movie theaters, and your... unique establishment. There is... absolutely nothing... for a chemical engineer. And by now, trying to find anywhere to work, our savings are almost completely gone."

I look at her pleadingly. She looks back at me with indecision.

"Please," I beg, before I realize the word was spoken aloud instead of just on repeat inside my mind.

I hold my breath.

Finally, she speaks. "The job pays ten dollars an hour plus commission. We're open from 10:00 a.m. to midnight Monday through Saturday and noon to six on Sundays. You split a schedule with my other girl, Ali. She works tonight at seven, so you can come figure out who gets which shift then."

I can't help the tears that spring to my eyes, but I don't let them fall. "Oh my gosh. Thank you so much. I promise you won't regret it."

"Oh, I know I won't, darlin'. You're obviously a hard worker. I just hope *you* won't," she tells me, and I nod, standing from the chair across from her desk as she does the same. "See you at seven."

"Yes, ma'am!"

I hurry out of the office, avoiding looking at the items on the shelves as I make my way to the glass door, hearing the bell jingle as I head to my car. As I pull open my driver side door, I glance over my shoulder at my new workplace, feeling a rush of excitement to get home to Astrid to tell her the good news.

"You are looking at the newest sales associate at Toys for Twats!"

Astrid, midsip, chokes on her coffee, setting her mug down on the thrift shop dining table as she covers her mouth with her hand. I wait for her to hack and dribble down her front before her coughing turns into laughter. My eyebrow rises as I cross my arms over my chest and cock a hip.

"My sister, one of the rising stars at a multi-million-dollar company that makes all-natural cleaning solutions, is now the sales associate of a sex shop?" Through her laughter, I see tears fill her eyes, but as her face slowly melts, I see they aren't happy ones, and my arms fall to my sides, all haughtiness dissolved. "I've ruined your life."

I rush forward and pull her to her feet, placing my palms against her now wet cheeks. I force her to meet my eyes, thankful the nasty bruise is finally gone from around her beautiful blue ones. "You did not ruin my life. You *are* my life, sis. You're worth everything." It's a mantra I repeat to her several times a day, the only thing I can think to do myself to help undo the emotional abuse her monster of an ex put her through for years.

"And as you're out busting your ass, trying to find anything to help us make ends meet, I'm the useless piece of shit sitting here doing absolutely nothing," she whimpers, and it makes me hate Brandon even more. My big sister, the beautiful, popular, extremely talented contemporary dancer back in high school, who I always looked up to and who always loved and included me, has been beaten down to a shell of the powerhouse she used to be.

"That's not true, Astrid. You're bringing in enough to pay for our groceries with your online makeup sales. You're putting food on the table. It was my idea for you not to go out and try to find a job. To keep you hidden as much as possible," I remind her.

"But how long until I have to shut that down? What if he finds out that I lied to my group followers? That Roberta Card isn't someone I recommended to them because I was quitting my makeup consulting and that it's actually still me? He could track me down!" The look of panic in her eyes makes me see red. "And if I do anything else, it's not like there are a million Astrid Quills in the world. A quick Google search and bam! He'd be here." She starts to tremble, so I force her to sit back down in her seat.

"He's not going to find you. We've got your stuff on lockdown. You've completely fallen off the grid. We're using all my information and accounts for everything. And it's not like he could know you're with me. I lived on the other side of the state. He never knew where I worked or anything, so he wouldn't be able to find out I've quit my job there and left with you if he doesn't know where to check," I assure her.

She sniffles and leans forward to wrap her arms around my waist from her seated position, resting her head on my stomach as she squeezes me. "All those times I picked on you for never having a boyfriend, for always burying yourself in your school work. And here, it's my saving grace that he won't have anyone to track you through. I'm sorry I always gave you shit for not taking the time to make friends, Twy."

"All I need is you." I stoop down in front of her and look up into her liquidy eyes. "And now with this fresh start, with my... interesting new job, maybe I'll finally take the time to do all that, yeah?"

She wipes her nose with the back of her shirtsleeve. "Yep. You promised. After you got all this set up for us, there's no more planning. We're living day by day from here on out."

"Exactly." I squeeze her knees. "Which means you, big sis, have to start putting the past behind you."

She nods, wipes away her tears, and puts in place her brave face. And then she looks at me oddly. "Um, Twy?"

"Yeah?" I tilt my head to the side.

"You know how I got into makeup consultation because, well, I know a lot about it and am really good at it?" she asks.

I squint, not knowing where this is going. "Yeeeah."

"Well... umm...." She starts to giggle. "How are you supposed to convincingly sell people naughty sex toys... when you're a virgin?"

Two

Seth

THE FAMILIAR SOUND OF THE DOOR'S bell jingling fills my ears as I walk into the local novelty store. I always get the club's supply of lube, toys, and things here, even though it would be cheaper to buy in bulk online. The guys and I decided it would be better to support one of our members' businesses. Plus, she gives us a bomb-ass discount anyways.

I grab a hot-pink basket from the stack, and without looking around, I head right for the wall of dildos, knowing exactly which ones we need. But before I can reach the colorful mass of phallic-shaped toys, I stop dead in my tracks as my path is intercepted by the most adorable creature.

"Well hello, there," I purr, taking in her shoulder-length shiny dark hair, framing a clean face that is lovelier than even the most professionally made-up ones I've ever seen. Her black-rimmed glasses perch on her slightly upturned nose, giving her a sexy librarian look. How lucky am I to have found her in a sex shop? Makes me wonder what she's here to buy.

"Welcome to... Toys for Twats. Can I help you find anything?" Her face flushes red, and it's not until I see her name tag that it clicks she's an employee, one I've never met before. All the others have been here for years and we know each other by name. My real name, Seth. Only the owner, Roxanne, knows my Dom name since she's a member of Club Alias, the BDSM club I own with my three partners.

"I have a list, actually," I tell her, pulling the folded paper out of the front pocket of my dark jeans. I hand it to her, watching closely as she reads the first item on the list.

She looks up at me, her brow furrowing. "Um, okay. Right this way."

I step forward, expecting her to turn in the opposite direction and head to the wall of dildos, but we end up colliding as she goes to walk around me in the direction from where I came through the door. A scent that is uniquely her, combined with her floral shampoo wafts up my nose, and my eyes nearly cross at how wonderfully intoxicating it is. So different from the leather and expensive perfumes I'm used to smelling every day. My dick twitches behind my zipper.

"Oh, gosh. I'm sorry. What you're wanting is right over there," she tells me, embarrassed, pointing over my shoulder.

It's not. Nothing on my list is over there. But color me intrigued. I want to know just what the fuck she's trying to take me to see. So I step out of her way and gesture for her to lead the way.

"Um, do you... are you wanting a certain, ah, size or anything?" she asks, and I have to fight to keep a straight face when I realize just what rack she's now standing in front of. I glance around, trying to see if Roxanne is playing a trick on me, but with no store manager in sight, I decide to see where this goes.

"No, I don't really have a preference. What would you suggest... Twyla?" I read the name on her badge. Such a unique name for such a beautiful woman. It fits her perfectly.

She clears her throat and looks up at me. "Well, ah, is... is the dildo for you or for your um... partner?"

I use every ounce of self-control I can muster not to burst out laughing. "It would be for my partner," I say seriously. I'm into some kinky shit, but dildos and butt plugs are not my thing when it comes to myself.

"Okaaay." She turns back to the rack and grabs a purple medium-sized, torpedo-shaped plug. "I would say, depending on what your partner is used to..." She glances down at the front of my pants and flushes crimson, her bright blue eyes widening behind her glasses before they meet mine. I can't help but smile. The glance might have been unconscious, but my hard-on inside my jeans is definitely not what she expected to find in her line of vision. She gracefully tries to ignore it. "I, uh... depending on what they're used to receiving in the bedroom, I guess you'd want to either, um... match it, or go bigger. Smaller, and they wouldn't really feel it. But I suppose you wouldn't want to go bigger, because then when it's just you again...." She looks absolutely horrified by the words coming out of her own mouth.

I put her out of her misery, take the butt plug from her hand, and place it in my pink basket. "Sounds good. All right, next on the list?"

She stares at the purple plug in the basket, either surprised she talked me into it or trying to figure out if the size of it actually matches the size of my cock. I refrain from informing her the toy's not even close.

"Twyla? The list?" I stoop down to catch her eyes with mine, snapping her out of it.

"Oh! Yeah, sorry." She fumbles with the paper and reads the next item. "Nipple clamps." Her head lifts as she glances around the store, her brow furrowing in confusion. "I'm not exactly sure we have those. Um, possibly over here." She heads to the back corner and stops before the display of bondage equipment. "Nipple clamps, nipple clamps," she mumbles, bending over to look on the lower hooks, giving me the perfect view of her incredible ass encased in black leggings. She pulls off a package of clothespins, flips them over to read the back of the label, and then replaces them on the hook. When she stands and faces me, she looks almost defeated. "I'm sorry, we must be out of them."

Hating the look of disappointment on her face, I tell her, "No biggie. Next on the list?"

She pushes her hair behind her ear, her face brightening when she sees what's written last. "Lube. We've got lots of that. Right this way." She hurries in the correct direction for the first time, and her posture lifts. "Do you know what kind you need? We have several brands, regular and flavored. Take your pick."

I look at the shelf of lubes, spotting the one I know I need for the club. Yet I'm not ready to end this time with the new sex shop employee who clearly knows nothing about the products she's supposed to sell. She must be a vanilla kind of girl. Either that, or she's never been with anyone who's shown her any adventure in the bedroom.

"What's the difference between water-based lubricants and the silicone kind?" I ask, and watch as her eyes fill with dread.

Damn. With how confidently she strode over here, I thought for sure maybe she had just been trained on these items and was excited to use her newfound knowledge. Wrong. She was obviously just happy she knew where something was located.

"I uh—"

"Seth, honey!"

Twyla and I both jump at the interruption. I had been so focused on her that I didn't see the shop's owner come out from the back office. I take a step back from her new employee and give her a grin.

"Rooooooooxanne!" I sing, belting it out so flawlessly Sting himself would applaud.

She strolls over and gives me a peck on the cheek before glancing into my basket. "Your load's a little light today, isn't it?" she asks.

"That's what she said," Twyla mumbles absently, and as all eyes turn to her, she slaps her hand over her mouth, looking like a deer caught in headlights. "I'm so sorry," she says from behind her palm. "It's a really bad habit my sister and I have."

Roxanne and I look at each other and then immediately burst out laughing.

"So you *do* have a sense of humor. Lord, I thought for sure these past few days that you wouldn't know a joke if one smacked you in your serious, pretty little face!" she tells Twyla. "Thank goodness. You can't work at a sex shop and not have a good sense of humor. Ain't that right, Seth?"

"No doubt," I reply, as Twyla lowers her hand, a small smile lifting the corners of her lips.

She breathes a sigh of relief. "Well that's reassuring. I seriously saw my job flying out the window. I mean, you'd think professionalism is key when you're trying to sell someone a dildo." She points into my basket.

Roxanne looks from Twyla, to the basket, then up to me, before doubling over, resting her hands on her knees as she laughs again. "God a'mighty, we've got some training to do," she manages to get out.

Twyla looks up at me then down to where Roxanne is still bent in half catching her breath, and then back up to me. And it finally dawns on her. "Wait, you know each other?"

"Seth here is one of our regulars," her boss explains.

Twyla cocks her head to the side, narrowing her eyes. I point down into the hot-pink basket dangling from my forearm. "Butt plug," I stage-whisper, and then point to the back wall. "The great wall o' dildos."

Judging by her earlier embarrassment, I wait for her face to heat, but this time, fire sparks in her eyes. "You were playing me the whole time?"

I grin. "I couldn't help it. Roxy hasn't had a new employee in the three years I've been coming here. When you tried to sell me a butt plug as a dildo, I just had to see what other comic gold I could get out of you."

The older woman giggles beside me. "Twyla, darlin', how did you not know the difference between butt plugs and dildos?"

The beauty before me huffs, flinging her hand in the direction of the wall of dildos. "I thought those were vibrators. That thing in his basket has like... a handle thingy on it." She makes a motion with her hand like she's grasping the handle of a bicycle tire pump and moves her arm back and forth, and I nearly die laughing when she says, "So you'd grip it like that and move it in and out of... wherever you decide to stick it."

When Roxanne and I finally catch our breath, we look at the new girl. I notice her rising discomfort, and then the panic in her eyes; it cuts my hilarity off at the quick.

"I'm a fast learner, Roxy. I promise I'll learn about everything and you won't have to worry about me messing up again. I really need this—"

Her boss waves her words away. "I have no doubt, honey. Don't you go getting all anxious. It was just a stroke of bad luck you had Seth here—the man who'd give Christian Grey a run for his money in the sex toy knowledge department—as your very first customer." Twyla nods, relief blanketing her delicate features. "Actually..." Roxy looks up at me, her eyes narrow and a smirk lifting the corner of her mouth. "It might not be bad luck at all. Seth, what do you say? You have your training sessions at the club. Could she attend some classes? Who better to learn her new trade from than a *master*?" She drawls out the last word.

"Excuse me?" Twyla inserts, clearly confused.

"As much as I'd love for her to be one of my students, the training sessions are for club members only," I sigh.

"Yeah, *official* training sessions... but what about private lessons? Say like... after club hours." Roxy wiggles her eyebrows.

My eyes take a long, slow stroll from the tips of Twyla's black Converse up to the single pin holding her dark hair back from her beautiful face, and I grin wickedly when I see her fidget in place. "I'd be down for that, if the lovely Twyla is game," I challenge.

She looks unsure, but Roxy cuts in. "You have an amazing opportunity right now, honey. The education Seth can give you would be like learning your chemistry stuff from the guy who invented the Magic Eraser himself. Pure genius, am I right?" She directs the question at me, and I shrug.

"What do you say, doll? Will you let me teach you? I promise I won't bite... until lesson three." I lick my lips, looking her directly in the eye.

And when she breathes, "Yes," and looks at her feet, I know she's all mine.

Twyla

DEAR GOD, BUT this man is freaking delicious. From the second we collided in front of the rack of flavored condoms, a dull ache had begun to take up residence between my thighs. He smelled so good, like leather and expensive cologne. And his body had been hard as a rock, completely opposite to his soft hazel eyes and friendly face. He was devastatingly handsome, with a closely cropped beard and thick eyebrows. Jesus, when he lowered those dark brows over those intensely bright eyes, looking up through his long lashes to give me that wicked grin, I swear... it clenched. My. Vagina. Clenched. It had been all I could do not to whimper and rub my legs together to relieve the tension.

And it's with these feelings coursing through my veins that I respond with an automatic "Yes" when Seth asks if he can teach me all about the things inside the store. I don't take into consideration the context clues between him and Roxanne. Something about a club? Training sessions? A master at what he teaches? Giving some guy named Christian a run for his money?

A regular in a sex shop, looking for dildos, nipple clamps, and lube?

All I know is when he said he'd love for me to be one of his students, and then looked at me with those mesmerizing eyes as he asked if he could be my teacher, I felt this undeniable urge to please him. I couldn't say no.

Plus, with my boss standing here telling me what a great opportunity it would be to learn all about her products, how terrible would it look if I turned them down? I need this job. If my sister's ex were to come looking for us, there's no reason he would ever consider checking here. In a way, leaving it up to fate placed us in the perfect spot. If Brandon ever worked out we'd left together, then certainly he would try to track us somewhere that my job as a chemical engineer would take us. And as we discovered, there's not a single place in town that my degree and job history would be of use. My new workplace is pretty much the best disguise we've got.

"Do you have Facebook?" Seth's voice cuts into my thoughts.

"Huh? Oh. No, I don't have any social medias," I reply, and see the familiar look of astonishment cross his face. It's the look everyone gets when I make the confession. "I used to have one, but once I got into college, I found all that stuff really distracting. I deactivated it so I could concentrate on my work. It was such a relief not feeling like I had to keep up with it that I never turned it back on."

"That's actually... kinda cool. I bet it's refreshing not feeling tied to your phone all the time," he says, and I blush at the praise. "Well, you at least gotta have an e-mail address, right?"

"Yes, it's easy. Twyla Quill at Gmail. I can write it down for you at the register," I respond, and he grins.

"As if your name couldn't be any cooler, you gotta go and add Star Lord to the end of it!" The excitement in his voice makes me smile coyly, but he must see the confusion on my face, because he prompts, "Star Lord? Peter Quill? Daaaaayum." He turns to

Roxanne. "She earned cool points for the *The Office* reference she let slip, but loses a few for not knowing *Guardians of the Galaxy*."

"Even I knew that one, and I hardly ever get your pop culture references," she mumbles, then chuckles at the look I'm giving them. "This man is fluent in movie and TV show quotes and song lyrics. It's like his second language."

"Dude! I just realized. We both have Chris Pratt character names! Yours is Quill, from *Guardians*, and he plays Owen in *Jurassic World*." He reaches his hand out and takes mine, the warmth of his palm spreading throughout my entire body. "Seth Owens, doll. Pleasure to meet you. I'll e-mail you times I'm available, and the address of my club."

If his flesh against mine didn't have me completely centered in this time and space, his squirrel moment would have given me whiplash. "Sounds good."

Then I watch in slow motion as he lifts my hand to his lips to press a kiss to my knuckles, and my heart pounds so hard behind my breasts my nipples harden. I don't know if it's the feel of his soft lips or the devilish look in his hypnotic eyes that makes me lose my breath, but I suddenly feel faint as everything around us disappears. It's not until he speaks again that the spell is only slightly broken.

"I look forward to it. But for now, I gotta grab my dildos, nipple clamps, and lube for the club," he tells me, humor lighting his handsome face.

"Take her along with ya, Seth. I've got an order to place in my office." And with that, Roxanne vanishes once again. Without letting go of my hand, Seth leads me to what I now understand is a huge wall of dildos.

"You seriously thought these were vibrators?" He looks down at me, his eyes twinkling.

I huff. "Well, they vibrate, don't they? Lots of them have remotes and settings." I gesture to the ones directly in front of us, obscene, vein-covered, penis-shaped toys that make me want to take a wide step in the opposite direction.

"Yes, but here's the thing. Vibrators are their own category. There are vibrating dildos, but not all vibrators are dildos," he explains.

I take a moment to absorb what he's saying. Seeing the confusion on my face, he lets go of my hand, and I immediately miss the connection but try to concentrate on what he says next. He reaches out to the left to grab a package, his muscular bicep bulging directly in front of my face as I get a whiff of his deodorant. Dear Lord, how can a man's deodorant even be sexy? Leather, expensive cologne, deodorant, and *him*. The combination is lethal. The crotch of my panties is officially soaked.

"This, lovely Twyla, is a vibrator. More specifically, it's a bullet. Some people like to insert it into either the vagina or ass, but mostly it's used for clitoral stimulation," he tells me, his voice unwavering. He obviously feels none of the tsunami of embarrassment that's crashing down on me. "Ah, none of that, doll. No need for pink cheeks around me. At least... not the ones on your beautiful face."

I gasp and take a step back, unsure if his innuendo is appalling or a total turn-on.

He chuckles, shaking his head, a wicked gleam filling his eyes once more. "This is gonna be a blast."

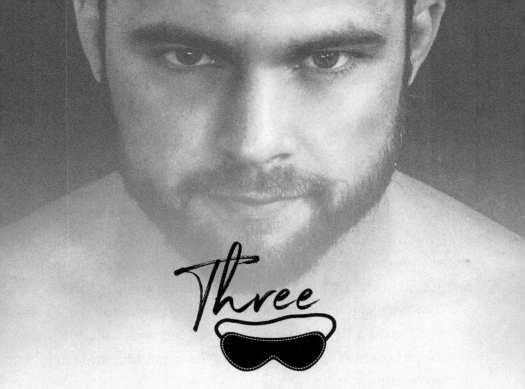

Three

Twyla

I STUMBLE THROUGH THE DOOR OF OUR apartment, drop my bag, and slip off my Converse before backing up to the couch. There, I fall backward, landing on the cushions with a plop. It's a nice, brown, ultrasuede sectional we got for an amazing price on Craigslist from a military family who was getting stationed in Germany. The perks of living next to an army base, I guess.

"Ya okay, sis?" Astrid asks from the other end of the L-shape.

My voice is low and monotone. "I mistakenly tried to sell a man a butt plug today when what he really wanted was six five-inch vibrating dildos. The most gorgeous man alive, I might add. Like, so sexy it hurt to look at him. And there I was, a twenty-four-year-old woman who barely knows the difference between massage oil and anal lube, trying to convince him I knew what I was talking about." I stare at the ceiling, picturing the scene in my head as my humiliation washes over me once again. "Turns out he owns a club and is a regular at the shop. Some kinda master at all things sex, according to my boss. And then, to make things even worse, Roxanne put me on the spot and set me up to learn about everything in the shop from him. 'Private lessons' at said gorgeous man's establishment. What sex toys and dance clubs have to do with each other, I have no clue."

I feel the cushions behind me tilt and readjust before my sister's pretty face appears above me, her arms bracing herself on either side of my head as she looks down at me.

"Twy. Are you trying to tell me you're going in to take lessons from a Dom at a BDSM club?" she asks, her eyes wide.

"No, his name is Seth, not Dom," I correct her, and she bites her lip before squinting at me.

"Oh, my sweet, nerdy little sister. You really have no clue, do you?" she asks.

My brow furrows as I glare up at her. "What are you talking about?"

"A *master* of all the products in a *sex shop*? Who owns a *club* and gives lessons on said products?" she confirms.

"Yeeeeah?"

"Twy, he's a Dominant. He owns a BDSM club. Come on, sis. You know, like Christian Grey," she prompts.

"There's that name again. Who is that dude? Apparently, my boss says Seth would give him a run for his money. He must be hot."

She gapes down at me. "Your lack of knowledge in all things pop culture never ceases to amaze me. But this? Sis, really? Christian fucking Grey. The delicious Dom in *Fifty Shades of Grey*, the global phenomenon. Not only are they books, but they're also movies now. You cannot tell me you've never heard of them!"

I remind her, "Astrid. I have no Facebook. No Instagram. No Myspace—"

"Myspace isn't a thing anymore. I mean, it is, but it's just for like... music or something," she cuts in.

"Whatever. I don't have any of those. I don't read the newspaper or watch TV, because it's always bad news that brings me down, and because I never have time. The last movie I saw in the theater was when you forced me to go with you to *Disturbia* in 2007 during your obsession with Shia Labouef phase." I pause to take a breath.

"Mmmmm, Shia." She smiles.

I roll my eyes. "*Anyway.* So no, big sis, I don't know who the hell Christian Grey is. While everyone else in the world was evidently reading about some super-hot B-D-whatever-you're-talking-about Dom dude, I was helping create a new formula for laundry detergent made of all-natural ingredients."

She plops back onto the couch, and I sit up to face her. "Wait... did you tell them the reason you know nothing about sex toys is not only because you never watch TV or movies, or read, or have any girlfriends who dish their naughty details, but also because *you're a virgin?*" she cries.

"How exactly would I have brought that up in conversation? 'Oh, B-T-Dubs, guys, I know you hired me at your sex shop, Roxy, but I haven't, in fact, ever had sex!' I would've basically been asking to be fired on the spot!"

"Well, that's true." Her face changes into a wicked grin. "That's all right though. Ana was a virgin for Christian too." When I give her a blank stare, she giggles. "When do you work next?" she asks.

"Wednesday."

"Two days. Okay. When are you supposed to meet your hottie?"

"He's not *my* hottie, and I don't know yet. I've got to check my e-mail because he's supposed to tell me where his club is and when he's available," I reply.

"Well until then, I'm giving you homework." She stands and hurries away, disappearing into her bedroom down the hall until she reemerges with her Kindle in hand. "You're not too busy now. Read the trilogy. And when you're done, I have several others you can enjoy."

I take the Kindle from her warily, looking at it as if it might burn me. "I never knew you liked to read."

She lowers her eyes as her happy face falls. "It's one of the only things Brandon let me do when I wasn't allowed to leave the house," she explains.

My heart sinks to my stomach. I don't know everything that went on in my sister's ten-year relationship, but the bits and pieces she told me were enough for me to formulate and execute the entire plan of getting her out of there. It took over a year of convincing her, but finally, even though I hated using guilt as a weapon against her, I put in my resignation and quit my job. After telling her there was no way to get it back because my position had been filled before my last two weeks were complete, she had no choice but to go along with my plan to help her escape. Her guilty conscience would allow for nothing else.

She clears her throat. "So, anyway, you've had a rough day, Twy. Go run yourself a bubble bath and start book one," she orders.

I nod, lumbering up from the couch. "Okay. What do you want to do for dinner?"

"Wanna split a frozen pizza?"

"Sounds good to me. I'll be out in an hour," I reply, noticing the smirk on her face. "What?"

"We'll see about that. I predict no less than three refills of hot water during your bath. It's *that* good." She wiggles her eyebrows, making me smile.

As I circle the couch, I lean down and plant a kiss on top of Astrid's head before making my way to my room. I grab the pajamas I plan on changing into after my bath, but when I turn to go to the bathroom, my laptop catches my eye. I wonder if Seth has e-mailed me yet. My phone died at work, so I haven't gotten any notifications if he did. Unable to fight the suspense, I set my clothes and my sister's Kindle on the bed before grabbing my computer off my nightstand. I hop up on top of my comforter and pull up my Gmail. And there, waiting for me in the inbox is an e-mail from Seven@clubalias.com.

Hello, Doll, it begins, and I smile. I've never been called a pet name before, and I kind of like it.

It was such a pleasure meeting you today, and I look forward to our first lesson. According to Roxanne, you have the day off tomorrow, so I figured why wait? Let's have our first class at 11:00 a.m. The faster I can teach you about the things in the shop, the faster you'll know what the hell you're selling. The club closes at 2:00 a.m., so that'll give me enough time to get a good night's sleep and to prep. Let me know if this time is good for you. I've attached the address and link to Google Maps so you can find the place.

Looking forward to seeing you again.

Seth Owens

My heart skips a beat at the thought of seeing him tomorrow.

I mean, I really have no excuse not to. And I do need to get some sort of grasp on the products so I don't make a fool of myself again. I reply before I can talk myself out of it.

Hi there, Seth,
Yes, 11:00 a.m. is good for me.

I watch the cursor blink for a full minute as I try to think of anything else to say, but I come up blank. I finish it up, deciding the quick response will have to be good enough.

See you tomorrow.
Twyla Quill

I close my computer and slip off my bed, grabbing my pajamas and the Kindle on my way out of my bedroom. I turn on the light in the bathroom and shut the door behind me, placing everything on the closed toilet lid before turning the water faucet on to fill the tub with scalding water. Call me weird, but I like to feel like a boiling lobster while I soak.

I squirt some of my Hello, Gorgeous bubble bath from Bath and Body Works into the water and watch as foam begins to form on the surface. I stand to pull off my black leggings, hot-pink Toys for Twats tee, and finally my underwear and bra, and then carefully step into the tub, holding onto the empty soap dish attached to the wall so I don't slip. I sigh as I lower into the steaming water, then reach over and grab the Kindle before lying back. I close my eyes and relax while the bathtub fills, and when I feel it reach the bottom of my neck, I turn off the faucet with my foot.

I flip the Kindle over in my hands, trying to figure out how to turn it on. When I finally manage to do that, I go into Astrid's library, scrolling through the different book covers until I find the one I've been assigned to read.

Five hours, three hot water refills, and four slices of pizza in the middle of my bed later, I only have two words, realizing what I've gotten myself into with Seth...

Oh my.

Seth

"I NEED TO run something past you guys, just to make sure y'all are okay with it," I announce inside my office at the club, after calling Corbin, Doc, and Bryan into the room.

It's a rare occasion they're all here at the same time. We are all a part of Imperium Security, accepting random bodyguard jobs here and there as a cover-up for our real operation. We're a mercenary team. For a substantial amount of money, someone can hire us to take care of a person... permanently. But we have a code. Someone can't pay us to murder just anyone. The hit must be a criminal who escaped justice, somebody who hired the right skeezy lawyers and had enough cash that they got away with something horrible. It's normally the family of a murder victim who hires us. We've worked on some pretty high-profile cases, but always make it look like an accident. No way to trace it back to us.

Club Alias was my brainchild. When our team was first formed by Dr. Neil Walker, our resident psychologist, we weren't sure how much work we would be pulling in. With no way to advertise our *real* services, relying on the smaller bodyguard jobs and word of mouth for our mercenary work, I wanted a backup plan. If everything fell through for Imperium Security, then I wanted something I knew for sure wouldn't go under. Sex and booze. They're two things that are just as certain as death and taxes: even in the worst economy.

"What's up, man?" Corbin prompts, sliding onto the leather couch against the wall. Bryan sits on the other end, and Doc falls into the leather chair in front of my desk, which I sit behind and pull my reading glasses off, setting them on my computer's keyboard. I had just finished reading Twyla's response to my e-mail and caught all the guys before they left for the night.

"Would any of you have a problem with me giving private lessons during nonbusiness hours here at the club?" I ask outright.

One of the things we take pride in is how strict we are with the rules of Club Alias. There's an entire process of gaining membership, and a hefty yearly fee, ensuring we only allow the most upstanding people into our establishment.

"Is a member unable to attend the regular training sessions or something?" Bryan questions.

"No, this isn't a member. I, uh... I met a girl at Roxy's shop," I confess, looking between all my coworkers. Just as I expected, their faces light with surprise.

"*You*... met a girl... outside the club?" Corbin inquires.

"I did." I nod once, meeting his eyes.

"You... Seth Owens... who hasn't been on a real date since I met you, who rarely even leaves this building except to go to the grocery store and sex shop, met a girl... outside the club?" Corbin clarifies.

"Dude. Yes. Now do you fucking mind if I bring her or not?" I gripe. I'm very well aware of my hermit ways.

Unlike Corbin and Bryan, I don't actually go on bodyguard jobs and mercenary missions. I'm the computer guru of the operation. The researcher. Anything technical the guys need, that's when they tag me in.

Doc speaks up, his usual sensible look in place. "I don't have a problem with it, as long as security cameras are still recording. You want to make sure to protect yourself, Seth, if you plan to be alone with her in one of the playrooms."

He has a good point. I don't know anything about Twyla. For all I know, she could call rape in the middle of a lesson, and I'd be unable to prove otherwise, leaving our entire business vulnerable. It wouldn't be the first time someone lied to get a settlement check from one of us after seeing how much money the club makes from membership fees.

"Agreed. First thing I'll do is have her sign the consent form to be recorded," I state, looking over to the guys on the couch.

Corbin chuckles. "I'd tell you to have your private lessons at your place, but ya kinda live here. I second what Doc said. As long as the cameras are rolling, I say go for it."

I flip him off. "Dude, as I've said a million times, the loft was empty, so why the fuck would I pay for another place to live when we already own the damn building?"

He puts his hands up in surrender. "Calm your tits, bro. Just giving you shit."

That leaves only Bryan, who gives me a stern look as he asks, "Who is this girl, Seth? Why doesn't she just apply for membership and take the official training sessions?"

"She's a new employee at Toys for Twats. She has no idea

what the fuck she's selling, but it seems she really needs the job, meaning she doesn't have the money for membership. I'm half doing it as a favor for one of our members, Roxy, who owns the shop, and half doing it, because...." I fidget in my seat, not wanting to hear any more shit from the guys.

"Because...?" Corbin draws out.

I growl in frustration. "I don't know, man. She made me feel... weird. And not in the made-my-dick-hard kind of way. Although she did that too. She's just... different. I don't know," I repeat.

Surprisingly, Corbin's face softens. "That's a good thing, bro. Very good. It's about time you felt something outside of lust for a chick."

I was definitely not expecting that from any of them, but I guess it makes sense coming from Corbin, who is living the good life, happily remarried to the love of his life, Vi, and expecting their first kid.

"In that case, I vote yes as well," Bryan says, standing and stretching his arms high above his head before letting out a huge yawn. "I gotta get some sleep." He moves to the door, calling over his shoulder, "Make good choices," his usual farewell to me, and disappears into the hallway.

Dammit, you play switch for a girl one damn time....

Corbin chuckles before standing to leave too. "I gotta get home to Vi. I ordered her to write four thousand words on her next novel, and let's just say I'm hoping she didn't make it. I've got a new riding crop I'm wanting to test out." He grins wickedly.

I laugh as he walks to the door. "How much longer until she pops? Don't send my bestie into labor, bro."

"Two months to go. I'll be gentle," he promises, and I shoo him out the door. It's so good to see the man I always knew as an emotionless killing machine so blissfully happy. Makes me wonder if I'll ever feel that way about a woman.

I face Doc, who's watching me closely. "Uh-oh."

"Excuse me?" comes his deep tenor.

"You're shrinking me. You've got your shrinky face on."

"I don't have a shrinky face," he mumbles, lowering his brows.

"You totally have a shrinky face, dude. You feel what your face is like right now? That's your shrinky face. Now go ahead and tell me what you're thinking. I know you're going to whether I want you to or not." I sit back in my chair and lace my fingers together, resting my hands on top of my abs and my elbows on the armrests.

"Seth, there's a reason we make all of our potential members go through therapy sessions before they are allowed in the club. You remember that, correct?"

"Yeees," I drawl. "But she's not trying to become a member."

"I'm aware. But I want you to take into consideration the things you want to teach this woman. Do you know anything about her background? Anything about her sexual experience? Have you thought about the fact you might not want to jump into the BDSM stuff like you would with a normal training session? Do you have any idea if she has any triggers? Her limits?" Doc questions, and it makes me pause.

He's right. I kinda just jumped into this. I'm so used to teaching these classes to people who have already been cleared by Doc during the therapy portion of the club's application process. With Twyla, I won't be handed a full report on my student. I won't know all of her sexual secrets before we begin.

"That's what I thought," he says, seeing the realization on my face. "You're supposed to be teaching her about the products in

Roxy's store, yes?" I nod. "So I would suggest a more hands-off approach. As you get to know her more, maybe the lessons will naturally progress from there."

I wilt a little, but I know he's got a point. "Good idea, Doc."

"Now, I'd like for you to expand on what you meant by she makes you feel 'weird,'" he tells me.

"And there's your shrink voice to go along with your shrinky face." I shift in my seat, but I know I can't just ignore him. One of the agreements all of us made when we signed on to this club together is we'd have regular sessions with Doc. In our line of work, the mercenary side more specifically, it wouldn't be safe for us to keep everything all bottled up.

I sigh. Might as well get this over with so I can get to bed sometime soon. "I ran into her at the novelty shop, where she's a new employee, as I said. She tried to sell me a butt plug thinking it was one of the dildos I was there to buy. I didn't correct her. That was fun and all because she was cute. But when she couldn't find the nipple clamps on the list, and then couldn't answer my simple question about lube, the look on her face...." I shake my head, not understanding the feeling that came over me. "It felt like a gut check to see her disappointment. Like she was mad at herself. And it made me kind of nauseous knowing I was the one to cause her to get that look."

He nods, looking pensive. After a silent moment, he does his Doc thing. "You don't get out much, Seth. Corbin was right. The only time you leave this building is to go buy food and to restock the toys for the club. You don't even own a car."

"Hey, I own a Harley," I insert defensively.

"Yes, and as badass as your bike is, even it is very telling. It's a single-seater. Leaving no potential for someone to ride with you. But you're not the norm for an introvert. You're not exactly a loner. You live here, where people come to *you*. You're constantly surrounded by your friends, by beautiful women. You have your choice of a different sub every night if you wish."

"Yeah, so?" I don't know what he's getting at.

"Let's backtrack. It's been a very long time since we had our initial therapy sessions. And maybe we can discover something that will explain the weird feelings you had with the girl from the shop," he says.

"Fuck, man. You already know everything about me. Do we really—"

"Yes." There's no room for argument in his tone.

"Fine. Where should we start?" I get up, walking over to the leather couch, and sprawl out. I kick my feet up on the armrest as I join my hands behind my head and stare up at the ceiling.

"At the beginning," comes his vague reply, and I roll my eyes.

"Yeah, yeah. Okay. What do you want from me, bro? How I was a child prodigy? How I graduated from high school at thirteen, and then was so much younger than all my peers all through my college years at MIT? You've been my psychologist since I was twenty when you swooped in with this crazy idea for the mercenary team. You're the one who taught me my urges to dominate weren't evil. That they sprang from never being around girls my own age, always being seen as their cute little nerd friend who they could use and cheat off." I don't like looking back at the first two decades of my life. It may sound really cool to be a real-life genius, but it was actually pretty fucking lonely.

"Let's revisit what I told you all those years ago, Seth. Your feelings of sadism were healthy in the fact you didn't actually want to hurt anyone. You wanted to feel in control. You wanted to be respected. You wanted to be heard. You were tired of being taken advantage of, mostly by girls who used the fact that you were going through college during puberty when they were already years into their womanhood. They were using their femininity to get something out of you during vulnerable years when you were maturing into the man you would become."

"Yeah, Doc. I've got all that. So what does that have to do with Twyla?" I know I'm grouchy, but I'm tired as hell and I really just want to go to my loft so I can get some sleep then wake up to see the beauty I made plans with.

"Twyla is the employee from the shop, I assume."

"Yup." Her image appears at the forefront of my mind. So sweet. So fucking beautiful.

"She's unlike the women you've submersed yourself in the past five years, yes?" he prompts, and I nod, closing my eyes. "Think of the all the submissives you've been with here at the club. Tell me what you see."

I sigh in frustration, but I give in. The faster I do as he says, the faster I'll get to bed. "Black leather. Tall stiletto heels. Perfectly made-up faces. All shapes and sizes, but all with an air of confidence that I helped put there for many of them through my training."

"Now, what do you see when you think of Twyla?"

"Sneakers. Comfortable leggings and a T-shirt. Thick-framed glasses resting on her adorable little nose in the center of her clean face. But she's even more beautiful than any of the girls at the club who put in hours of primping. Yet there's no air of confidence. She's unsure. Seems vulnerable somehow," I list quietly, really thinking about her first impression.

"What do we always say about submissives?" he asks, more like a reminder.

"Submissives are the ones who are actually in control of a scene. They have the power to call out their safe word and end a sexual act. The Dom has no choice but to end it because the sub is the one *allowing* the domination," I recite.

"It sounds to me like Twyla's vulnerability spoke to you. You didn't like her feeling disappointed in herself. And you didn't like sensing you were the one who made her feel that way. As much as you like to dominate and feel respected, you also like making submissives feel their potential power. You're a good person, Seth. You like lifting people up. By offering to teach Twyla about the things at the shop, you are giving her a sense of power through knowledge," he explains, and it makes sense. Yet...

"But that doesn't explain why she made me feel weird."

"Well, I thought that'd be obvious. It's the first time you've gotten the urge to empower someone outside the club. You're not wanting to give her sexual power. You're wanting to give her strength to use in the real world. And there also might be more to it than that as well."

"What do you mean?" I ask, turning to look at him. He's sitting comfortably in the leather chair in front of my desk.

"Something unexplainable. Look at Corbin and Vi. Would you say there is some unexplainable draw between the two of them, something that can't be broken down into exact reasons why they just... fit?"

I stare back up at the ceiling, thinking of my best friend and his wife. It's true. You can't put your finger on it. But for some reason, there's no doubt the two are meant to be together. They complete each other. Soul mates. And they claim they felt it the moment they met.

"And with that, I'll let you get to bed. Seems you've got an exciting day ahead of you," Doc says, patting my elbow as he passes me on his way out the door.

Four

Twyla

TURNS OUT CLUB ALIAS WAS WITHIN walking distance of my apartment. Makes me wonder how many people in the relatively quiet town know there is a place made specifically for sexual debauchery right under their noses.

When I arrive at the building, there are two doors. The one on the left is a glass door with the words Imperium Security in bold lettering, along with a phone number and business hours. The door on the right is painted black and unmarked. I look around, seeing no other entrance, so I pull on the handle to the unmarked one, gasping a little in surprise when it opens. I thought for sure it would be locked for some reason, even though Seth knows I'm coming at this time.

Inside, there is a small foyer with a host stand, but no one in sight. Beyond that, there is only a set of stairs that continues up until you can't see where it leads. With nowhere else to go, I head up the stairs.

Reaching the top, I look around the giant open area. There is a horseshoe of leather booths around a huge dance floor with two bars on either side of it. Around the perimeter of the entire space, there are framed alcoves like open rooms, but from where I stand, I can only see the ceilings of each one, since the booths have high backs, blocking the view inside.

Directly to my right, there is a metal staircase leading up to a door, which opens just as my eyes land on it. Out steps Seth, and I watch as he gallops down the stairs, a smile on his face when he reaches the bottom and starts making his way over to me. I have time to take in his dark jeans, and black long-sleeved Henley stretched taut over his muscular frame just before he stands in front of me.

"Good morning, doll," he says cheerily, his voice sounding loud in the silent, wide-open space.

"Morning," I reply softly, feeling like I should be quiet in the almost ominous feeling place. I've never been to a dance club before, much less during the day, and even less a club made for teaching the things I just read about in Astrid's romance novel last night. Maybe it would feel less imposing if it were full of people using the space as it was made for. I get the sense I'm somewhere I'm not supposed to be, like that eerie feeling you get when you stay after school. The empty halls and classrooms always used to creep me out when I'd stay to tutor someone after the last bell rang.

"Before we get started, I have something for you to read and sign. It's the same contract all our members sign. It just states that you're aware there are security cameras throughout the entire club, including in the playrooms. They're there to ensure everyone, employees and patrons, are protected," he explains, leading me to one of the large leather booths next to one of the bars.

Playrooms? Oh, God. This is for real. I guess I thought everything in the book was just fantasy, something made up, like a sci-fi novel or whatever, and when I got here, it would just be a regular old bar with naughty pictures in the bathrooms. But no. This is a real-life BDSM club. One that apparently has cameras in its playrooms for security. At first, the idea of being watched on a security camera freaks me out, but I suppose if you're already here and have the balls to do these... acts out in the open anyway, then you really wouldn't care if someone was watching it happen on a screen somewhere.

I slide into the booth but then keep on scooting over when Seth sits beside me instead of on the other side. His nearness is intoxicating. The scent of leather is much stronger here than when I smelled it at the shop, and being in his environment, I see why he carried the aroma with him. The feel of his body so close to mine is scorching. I could slide away a little more, but the heat is somehow comforting, the same way my scalding baths make me feel.

Handing me a pen, he lays the contract on the tabletop, and before I can stop it, a very unladylike snort escapes me. I bite my lip, knowing he's staring at me. I can feel his eyes heating the side of my face. I timidly turn my head, meeting his breathtaking gaze.

"What's funny, doll?" he asks quietly, his face so close to mine I can smell the blueberries he must've eaten for breakfast.

"I, uh... this isn't a contract asking me what my hard limits are, is it?"

A smile spreads across his handsome face, and I can't help but admire his straight white teeth, framed beautifully by full lips and his brunette beard, a few shades darker than his hair, which is perfectly, purposely disheveled atop his head.

"Did someone do a little research after work yesterday?" he teases, looking almost... proud.

"As a matter of fact, I did. My sister made me read her copy of *Fifty*. It was... enlightening," I admit, trying not to let on just how much I'd enjoyed it.

He throws his head back, letting out a belly laugh. It's infectious, and I can't help but giggle. "You had never read it before?" he gets out when he catches his breath. When I shake my head, his brow furrows, but his smile is still in place. "First *Guardians of the Galaxy*, and now this? What rock have you been living under?"

"No social medias, remember? For the past ten years, I've been doing absolutely nothing except school and work. Trust me, my sister gives me enough shit about it," I grumble, rolling my eyes.

"What did you go to school for?" he asks.

"Chemical engineering. And for the past two years, I've been on a team in California working on all-natural cleaning solutions. I was allergic to a lot of stuff growing up, and my mom had this book, the *Encyclopedia of Natural Medicine*. Instead of bedtime stories, I would fall asleep reading pages of that book. I found it so interesting that something that came from the earth could be just as effective, if not more so than the stuff we'd buy at a grocery store or pharmacy with all those chemicals in them. I grew out of a lot of my allergies, but the book always stuck with me," I explain. It's the most personal conversation I've had with another human being since, well, ever.

He tilts his head to the side. "A chemical engineer, who doesn't like chemicals, and who now works at a sex shop."

"That's me." I shrug. "What about.... Oh, never mind." I fiddle with the pen he'd handed me, dragging the contract closer so I can read it.

"What? What were you about to ask?" When I shake my head and continue to read the contract, he reaches up, takes hold of my chin, and turns me to face him. I hear myself gulp when I meet his eyes once again. "What were you about to ask?" he repeats, and his tone is more of a demand than a question, making my heart flutter inside my chest.

"I was, um, just going to ask about you. How does one open a BDSM club? But you don't have to—"

"I was also super into school. Believe it or not, I'm a fucking genius." He grins, wiggling his eyebrows. I think he means metaphorically genius, for opening up a BDSM club when it's apparently so mainstream now, but then he explains he means literally. "I graduated high school when I was thirteen, then college at MIT when I was twenty with my masters in computers."

There is complete honesty in his tone and eyes, and all I can do is blink up at him. "A prodigal child, master in computers, who now owns a BDSM club."

"I guess you could say I went from being a master at computers to a master of tapping dat ass," he tells me, and I burst out laughing. "There it is. That's the smile I wanted to see," he says gently, pushing a strand of hair behind my ear before tracing my jawline with his fingertip, sending a shiver up my spine and instantly hardening my nipples.

I don't know what to do or say. I feel like I've been frozen in place, even though my body feels like it's suddenly caught fire.

"Don't ever be afraid to ask me anything, doll," he implores, and my face softens as I nod. "Okay, look over the contract and sign. I'm excited to get started."

"Why do you call me that?" I ask, using his fancy pen to scrawl my name across the line on the last page.

"What? Doll?" he clarifies, and when I nod once again, he simply states, "Your name is Twyla," before sliding out of the booth.

I scramble after him, following as he walks around the row of booths and past the open alcoves I can now see are the playrooms he mentioned. I try not to look too closely, completely intimidated by what I glanced in the first one, which appeared to be a wooden cross with shackles attached to each end. "What does my name have to do with a doll?" I question, but all he does is chuckle as I see him shake his head from behind.

"You really have no pop culture knowledge, do you?"

"We've established this," I huff, and then almost run into him as he abruptly stops in front of the first playroom on the back wall of the club.

"It'll be like I'm speaking a foreign language to you. This should be interesting." He looks down at me when I walk around him. When he gestures for me to precede him into the room, I do a side-eye peek inside and then face him. I'm sure my expression shows nothing but panic. "Aw, no need to be afraid, lovely Twyla. I'll be gentle."

But the wicked grin on his face doesn't match his softly spoken words.

He takes my hand and pulls me into the room. "Sit there," he instructs, pointing to a black leather chair against the left wall. As I do, I watch as he pulls over a rolling table that has a plethora of toys I recognize from the shop, and my face instantly heats. He chuckles. "Hopefully by the end of all this, you'll be able to see this stuff without blushing. It'll be a shame though, since it's fucking adorable."

"I doubt I'll ever be comfortable with this stuff," I murmur, sitting back in the seat, getting as far away from the devices as I can get without becoming one with the wall.

He puts his hand to his heart. "Now what kind of teacher would that make me? By the time I'm done with you, you'll be a master at dildo hocking."

His grin makes me smile. He has a way of distracting me from my discomfort and making this awkward situation more fun. I'll give him that much.

"All right. Before we begin, I need to ask you some personal questions. That way I can assess what you already know, or decide if I need to start all the way down at the basics. No, no, no. Get that 'I'm about to run for my life' look off your face, young lady. I had a feeling you aren't much of a sharer, so in return, I will give you something I've never given another one of my students before. And it may not sound like much, but it really fucking is."

This piques my interest enough to battle back my fight-or-flight instinct that he was obviously able to pick up on. "And what's that?" I prompt.

"The power to ask me personal questions too. Like I said in the booth, ask me anything you want, Twyla. This isn't a normal situation for me. You are literally the first person who has been in one of my playrooms who wasn't a full-fledged member of the club. There are very strict rules here, ones I had to clear with my partners last night just to be sure we were all okay with breaking just this once. Just for you." His voice comes out soft at the end, making me feel warm inside.

"Thank you, Seth," I say quietly, not wanting to disturb the sweet moment. "No one's ever gone to so much trouble for me before."

"It's no trouble at all, doll. I wouldn't be doing this if I didn't want to. But that brings us to our first rule of the club. I'd insert a *Fight Club* joke here, but you wouldn't get it, so I'll skip that part." He chuckles. "When we are here, at Club Alias, you must refer to me as Seven. Right now, you'll only be coming during nonbusiness hours so you won't be around any of the members or staff. But in the event you want to become a member, it would be best if you got used to calling me Seven in this environment, so you don't slip up and reveal my real name to anyone."

"So *that's* why your e-mail address said Seven. I was wondering about that. What's with the codenames? Or is it a nickname?" I question.

"Keeping everyone's identity secret here is very important. The people who can afford membership are those who wouldn't exactly want their patients, or clients, or anyone else knowing the kinky shit they're into. Besides Roxy, who has signed a confidentiality agreement, and my partners, you are now the only other person on the face of the planet who knows that I, Seth Owens, am Seven, Dom and co-owner of Club Alias."

As he stares into my eyes, I can feel him searching... wondering if I'm trustworthy enough to keep his secret. I can't even measure what a big deal this is for him, and the fact he's given me this vital information about him makes me trust him too.

"I... I'll take it to the grave. I promise... Seven," I tell him honestly.

He walks up to my chair, puts one hand on each of the padded armrests, and leans down, his face mere inches away from mine. "Care to seal it with a kiss, doll?"

My heart leaps up into my throat. His eyes... God, his eyes are so fucking beautiful. So many blues, greens, and gold swirled together. And they twinkle with both heat and challenge. And for the first time in my life, I *want* to kiss a guy. Sure, there was that one time in middle school when James Justinson ran up and planted one on me in the hallway between classes after his friends dared him to kiss the first girl he spotted, but that totally doesn't count.

Yet, with my hesitation, he must think I don't want to. And like the good guy I'm discovering him to be, he smiles gently and then reaches up to push my glasses up into place with his pointer finger before softly tracing down the bridge of my nose. The caress is sweet, yet the most intimate thing that's ever transpired between me and another person. And I miss his proximity when he stands up and backs away.

I clear my throat, sliding back down into the seat. "Um, so uh. Where did you get the name Seven?" I ask, trying to get back on track.

He chuckles. "I don't suppose the only show you've watched besides *The Office* happens to be *Friends*, is it?"

I shake my head. "Nope. But I've never watched *The Office* before either."

"But... then how would you know about the 'That's what she said' thing?" he questions.

"My sister says it all the time to make me laugh, and it just kind of stuck. I didn't know she got it from a TV show. I thought she was just making everything sound dirty," I confess.

He lowers his face into his palm, and his shoulders begin to shake with laughter. Finally he sighs, his grin firmly in place. "What am I gonna do with you?" After a moment, he gets back to my original question. "I'll tell you what. If you can make it through this lesson and learn what I've planned for the day, I will show you where my Dom name came from."

"Deal," I agree.

"Okay, so, first personal question. Have you ever used *any* sex toy before, with another person or by yourself?" he asks, completely straight-faced.

"That would be a negative," I reply, proud of myself for being able to reply without being embarrassed.

"So I assume you only use your fingers to pleasure yourself." He hops up on the edge of the padded table directly across from me, his black boots dangling a foot off the ground.

"Um... no. Not exactly," I say, trying to keep my nerves under control.

"Look at me, Twyla," he says, his voice taking on a commanding tone that instantly snaps my eyes up to his from his boots. It does something funny to my belly. "First and foremost, there is no judgment here. I will never judge you for the things you like or want. I will never think differently of you for your past experiences. You could tell me you like to throw your stilettos at men's genitals while they thank you and call you princess, and I wouldn't bat an eye."

He ignores my snort and continues, "But what I will not tolerate, if you truly want to learn, is not being open with each other. Normally, when I'm in this room with another person, training them, I already know every single thing about them. They have to go through weeks of therapy with our resident psychologist to be cleared before they're ever allowed to be in the building. I need to know these things for both of our safety. For example, we have a submissive who is a rape survivor. She had triggers. Something that we could've easily been doing for pleasure for someone else, on her, they could have sent her into a state of panic, or worse. Much, much worse."

I stare into his eyes, feeling his seriousness like a tangible thing. Being so used to his lighthearted and jovial ways, the gravity of what he's telling me hits me deep. Can I do this? Can I let down my walls and allow him to get to know more about me than anyone else, even more than my sister?

Maybe if I look at this like any other class I've taken, one of my courses at school, then I'll be able to learn everything without it feeling too personal. And for some reason, I trust him when he says he won't judge me. Even though I don't know if I'm quite ready for him to know there's really nothing to tell about my past.

I clear my throat again, keeping my eyes on his when I speak. "Normally, I use my showerhead to masturbate. I've never been comfortable touching myself, so I always use the concentrated setting on my showerhead when I need... relief."

There, I said it. My voice unwavering and everything. I'd give myself a pat on the back if it weren't such a nerdy thing to do.

And just as he promised, Seven doesn't say anything to make me regret my confession. Instead, he stands from the padded table, quickly adjusts the sudden tent at the front of his pants without shame, and makes his way to the rolling table full of toys.

"That's a good place to start." He hands me a small purple device, phallic in shape, but doesn't look like a replica of an actual penis. It's smooth and pink, and at the end, there is a ring around it. "Spin the end just one click," he instructs. I do as he says, and it comes to life, vibrating gently. "That is a waterproof vibrator. Some people enjoy them in the shower or bathtub, or anywhere else where it would be submerged. A lot of women cannot orgasm off sex alone, and they need a little something for clitoral stimulation. That little guy would be perfect for sex in a pool, or even if you're not going into water. Turn it up another notch." I spin it one more click, feeling the vibration get stronger. "Now, touch it to your nose."

"Like, seriously?" I pull my eyes away from the device to see if he's being funny.

He's not.

"This is a trick you can use at the store. You don't want your customers sticking vibrators between their legs to test out how strong they are. Touch it to your nose, and it's a good indicator just how powerful it'll feel on your clit," he explains.

Feeling silly, but determined to learn everything I can, I place the end of the vibrator against the tip of my nose, pulling it away quickly when it tickles. "That feels way stronger than it did just in my hand." I giggle.

"Neat trick, huh? Little guy's got some power." He smiles.

"That's what she said," I murmur, turning the device off and hearing him chuckle.

"Now, check this one out." We trade toys, him handing me a tiny silver toy the size of a bullet, attached to a cord with a remote control. "Hold the vibrator in one hand, and the remote in the other." I do as he says. "Good. Now, click the button one time."

When I push the button, the little bullet comes to life, and dear God the thing buzzes so hard I nearly drop it. "Holy crap!"

"Right? And that's on the lowest setting. Click it again, going through the different settings, until it stops again," he instructs.

I work my way through the different strengths and patterns of vibrations until it finally reaches the end. "But wouldn't this one be hard to hold on to with it being so small?"

"It actually makes it nice to use with a partner. There's not a big, bulky object you're trying to get between your bodies in order to get the stimulation. A woman could easily hold that in place while her lover takes her from the back or the front. A lot of larger vibrators, there isn't much room for it during missionary and can only be used in other positions, like doggy style, where the other's body wouldn't be blocking the device from the clit. Which brings me to my personal favorite...."

When he hands me the pink device, my eyes widen. "Where the hell does this thing go?"

He laughs, walking back over to the padded table to sit down. "Bring it over here," he orders, using that sexy tone again that makes me want to do anything he pleases.

So I stand and make my way over to him. He spreads his knees and pulls me closer by my hips until I'm standing between his muscular thighs. My heart pounds in my chest as my stomach fills with butterflies being this close to him. His hands rest at my waist, practically burning me through my clothes.

"It's not what you're thinking. This, lovely Twyla, is the Wild Orchid. Yes, it looks like there are two shafts, one shorter than the other, but it is not meant to fill both holes," he says, and this time I *do* blush. "The longer, bulbous one is inserted into your pussy, and when it's all the way in, the shorter one will naturally rest on top of your clit. Place your hand around the longer one, letting your fingers rest beneath the short one. There you go, and now, when I turn it on...."

He squeezes the end of the device, where a button must be hidden beneath the rubbery surface, and when it comes to life, my knees grow weak imagining what that would feel like between my legs.

"Wow," I breathe, and then bite my lip.

"Yeah." And then after a moment, he says, "Would you like to try it?"

My eyes snap to his, surprised at his suggestion.

He chuckles. "As much as I would fucking love to try it on you, I meant would you like to take it home and test it out yourself."

I try not to think about why I feel disappointed that he wasn't offering to show me exactly how to use it properly, and instead say, "Oh, that's okay. I can imagine."

He squeezes my hips between his thighs, reminding me just how close our bodies are pressed. "Why imagine when you can experience?" His voice is molten, making my core clench, and I'm suddenly regretting not wearing any panties with my leggings today. "This is a brand-new toy, right out of the package. No one has ever used it before, if that's what you're worried about."

"No, no. It's not that." Shit, should I tell him now? I guess I need to. "I've just never—"

"I know, doll. That's why I'm offering you to take it home so you can try it out in privacy. Watch." He takes the toy from me in his right hand and makes an O-shape with his fingers and thumb of his left. "You just take the longer one's tip, and slowly slide it inside you. And once you've got it in place, you won't even need to move it in and out. Just tilt the back end of it down toward your ass, which will press the other end against your G-spot, and—"

"No, I mean—"

"I don't think you'll fully appreciate how awesome the Wild Orchid is unless—"

"It'll hurt!" I squeak, finally getting his attention.

"Not if you're gentle. Don't just go shoving it in there, doll,"

he says, not understanding. And why would he? He has no idea
I'm...

   "I'm a virgin."

Five

Seth

"A VIRGIN," I TELL DOC, PACING THE floor of his office after calling for an emergency appointment. "What am I supposed to do with that, man?

"Who says you have to do anything with it, Seth?" he asks, watching me from his leather seat.

"I've never taken anyone's virginity before. All my peers growing up were way older than me, always more experienced. I lost mine to a chick four years my senior. And then at the club, well... you know. People don't exactly join a BDSM club when they haven't even lost their V-card yet," I ramble, driving my hand through my hair in frustration.

"Who says you ever will? You're getting way ahead of yourself here." His tone is annoyingly calm. "Why don't you sit down? Relax. Let's talk this through."

I growl, throwing myself onto his couch like a toddler having a tantrum.

"Now, am I right in my assumption that the weird feelings you mentioned before have continued since getting to spend more time with Twyla?" Doc asks.

I sigh, knowing he's going to make me walk through this with baby steps. "Yes."

"Would you say the weird feeling has lessened, stayed the same, or grown?"

"Well, up until the second the word virgin left her mouth, it was definitely growing. Like, out-of-control growing," I admit.

"But after?" he prompts.

"I don't know. It's like this bucket of ice-cold water got dumped inside my gut. I'd never felt that before, so I have no idea what it means. It freaked me out for sure."

"What did you do when she told you?"

"You know I have a poker face that wins me the pot when I don't even have a pair on the table. I didn't want to hurt her feelings or make her feel bad in any way, especially after the way seeing her disappointment that first day at the shop made me feel. So I carried on the lesson as if it wasn't a big deal," I reply, giving myself a pat on the back for how I was still able to teach her about three more types of dildos—while internally having a panic attack—before she left and I immediately rode here, calling Doc on my way.

"Very good, Seth. Believe it or not, that shows a level of maturity needed for a real relationship. Taking her feelings into consideration above your own, instead of automatically reacting, that was impressive."

"Don't patronize me, Doc. I'm not an asshole. Of course I

wouldn't make someone feel like shit for something like that," I grumble.

"I'm not patronizing you. I'm being completely serious. Think about it. For the past five years, you've been a Dom at a club you own. If anyone says or does something you don't like or agree with, you have the power and the right to punish them as you see fit. It's expected of you. You know some of those subs even do it on purpose, just to receive your discipline," he reminds me. He's got a point.

"I had to be stern with her a couple times. I'm not used to having students reluctant to learn," I insert.

"Yeah? And how did she react? Not knowing if she's a submissive personality or not, I'm curious."

"Sexy flush. Panted breaths. Crossing and uncrossing of her legs. She even bit her lip. There was no defiance whatsoever. And she responded to it immediately," I tell him, picturing the beauty in my head and remembering how I had wanted to order her to do much more than be open and honest with me.

"What else can you tell me about your afternoon with her?" he asks, jotting something down on his ever-present notepad.

"Well, at first I thought we had nothing in common. She doesn't watch TV or movies, so she doesn't get any of my jokes. Which is different for me. Challenging. She's very serious, so when I can make her laugh, I feel like I've accomplished a feat. She doesn't fake her laughter. She doesn't just do it like a lot of the women at the club do. That flirtatious annoying giggle they do, thinking it'll stroke my ego. She doesn't do that."

"You like her genuineness, her authenticity," he tells me, doing his Doc thing. He can always take tidbits of shit I say and wrap them up into one simple explanation.

"Exactly. I like that." I nod.

"Okay, now. You said 'at first' you thought you had nothing in common. Did you learn something about her to change your mind about that?" he asks.

"Yeah, she's brainy. Like super smart. She was a chemical engineer before she moved here. Was really focused in school, a lot like me."

"Hmm... interesting," he murmurs, stroking the lines of hair on either side of his lips. "Why would a chemical engineer need a job at a sex shop?"

"I'm not sure. I didn't even think to ask. She's new in town, moved here with her sister, and just said she really needed the job." I shrug. "But she said she's never had much of a social life, which explains why she's still a virgin. She doesn't even have Facebook, bro."

"Imagine that." He snorts. A very un-Doc-like thing to do.

"What? What's that look for?" I sit up, narrowing my eyes at him.

He leans forward, bracing his elbows on his knees, and stares me in the eye. "You like her authenticity, her honesty. And... check this out. She's a woman that you, the real-life genius, could actually hold an intelligent conversation with." He sees the way I'm mulling that over, because he asks, "When was the last time you actually held a real conversation with a woman that wasn't about sex or having movie quote battles?"

I think about it... hard. "Not since I've opened the club. Probably college."

He nods slowly, stroking his beard in thought. "I believe I've got it."

"Got what?"

"The reason you're freaked out over her virginity."

"Well, let's hear it. Everything else you've untangled makes sense, so I've got to hear this," I urge.

"At the club, to you, there's nothing really special about the submissives. There's a sea of them, and you pick a different one each time you want to act out a scene or get your rocks off. There's always a different student to teach. And they're already primed and ready. They're literally at the club for sex, nothing more. And to them, you are just one of many Doms. You like it that way. No one gets attached. It's just sex for everyone involved. If it's good, then it may be memorable. But it's just another face in the crowd." He leans back, placing his ankle on the opposite knee. "But that wouldn't be the case with Twyla. She's a virgin. Everyone remembers their first. That, and she's not technically a submissive. When was the last time you made love to someone? Not only that, when was the last time you just had normal, vanilla sex?"

"Um, never. The chick I lost my virginity to wanted me to choke her," I state.

"And there we have it."

"Have what?"

"You're just as much a virgin as she is. It's not *her* virginity that freaks you out. It's yours. You're a Dominant. A Master at sex. You spend your nights teaching people all about physical, sexual pleasure. And if you want to be with Twyla, who you obviously have feelings for, which you've never felt before, then you will have to be the one learning something new. How to make love for the first time. How to have sex with emotion."

I ponder this for a solid minute, nothing but Doc's antique clock ticking away the seconds in the otherwise silent room.

Finally, I look up at my friend, throw out my ego, and ask with total sincerity, "Where do I start?"

Twyla

I GOT HOME from work about an hour ago, and for once, I don't feel like a failure. I was able to sell each customer who came into the store at least one of the products Seth taught me about yesterday, including two Black Orchids, which is one of the more expensive items we sell. Meaning, I'll make a nice amount of commission off them. I even got each to touch the vibrators to their noses, and just like Seth said, it was a cool trick that made them *oh* and *ah* over the power of the vibes. Plus, it was pretty funny to watch.

Seeing I have an e-mail from Seth, I sigh in relief. I had this fear that after I told him I was a virgin, I'd never hear from him again. The sensible part of me said that fear came from being a student not wanting her teacher to give up on her. I mean, would he find me a hopeless pupil? Too amateurish to bother with? The more fantastical part of me said the fear came from being an inexperienced woman. Would he find me less attractive knowing I wasn't as well versed in sex as the women he's used to? And it's this side of me speaking up that makes me realize: I want him to want me. Because I think... no, I know—yep, definitely, for sure—I want him.

I open up the e-mail to distract myself from my confusing thoughts.

From: Seven@clubalias.com
Subject: Congrats! You completed Lesson 1

As promised, doll, here is the reason my Dom name is Seven.
Enjoy.

Attached is a link to a YouTube video titled *"Friends – 7 Erogenous Zones by Monica."* I click it and watch as the three-minute-and-ten-second clip starts to play. I recognize the characters. My dad used to watch this show all the time. I can remember catching bits and pieces of it while I'd be doing my homework, sitting on the floor in front of the coffee table while he watched TV.

In this scene, Monica, the brunette chick, and Rachel, the one with the great hair, are sitting on their couch, talking to Chandler, one of the other main friends.

Monica (to Chandler): So, did you do it?

Chandler: (disappointedly) Yes, yes, we had the sex.

Monica: Uh-oh, was it bad?

Chandler: It was fine, you know, but she didn't agree with me as strongly as she agreed with Joey. She was more like, uh, "Oh, I see your point. I'm all right with it."

Monica: Well, it was the first time. You know, there's not always a lot of agreement on the first time.

Rachel: Yeah, not for girls anyway. Guys agree (snaps her fingers) like that.

Chandler: Look, you have to help me, okay? I mean, I know what to do with a woman. I know where everything goes. It's always... nice. But I need to know what makes it go from "nice" to "My God, somebody's killing her in there!"

Monica: All right, I'm going to show you something a lot of guys don't know. Rach, hand me that pad over there. (Rachel gets a notepad and pen off the table and hands it to Monica.) All right. Now... (starts to draw)

Chandler: You don't have to draw an actual wo— (looks down at Monica's drawing) Whoa, she's hot!

Monica: Now, everybody knows the basic erogenous zones. You got, (starts labeling her diagram) one, two, three, (Chandler nods impatiently), four (now Chandler looks up, surprised), five, six, and seven.

Chandler: (shocked) There are seven?

Rachel: Let me see that. (looks at the drawing) Oh yeah.

Chandler: (points to diagram) That's one?

Monica: (chuckles) Kind of an important one.

Chandler: Oh, you know what? I was looking at it upside down.

Rachel: Well, you know, sometimes that helps.

Monica: Okay, now, most guys will hit one, two, and three, and then go to seven and set up camp.

Chandler: And that's bad?

Rachel: Well, if you go to Disneyland, you don't spend the whole day on the Matterhorn.

Chandler: Well you might if it were anything like seven.

Monica: All right, uh... the important thing is to take your time. You want to hit them all and you want to mix them up. You got to keep them on their toes.

Rachel: Oh, toes! (raises hands in air. They both look at her.) Yeah, for some people. (Chandler looks at her feet and then back up to her face, raising a brow.)

Monica: Okay, you could, uh, start with a little one; a two; a one, two, three; a three; a five; a four, a three-two; a two, a two-four-six; (Monica starts to get into it) two-four-six; four, (Rachel moves back and stretches out) a two; (Monica now has her eyes closed and is getting visibly excited) two; four-

seven; five-seven (Chandler looks away from both of them as if he can't believe what's happening); six-seven; seven, seven, (faster) Seven, seven, seven. Seven. Seven. Seven. (Chandler looks at her in disbelief as she cries out) Seven! Seven! *(Monica, eyes still closed, leans back, shudders, and says silently, while holding up seven fingers)* Seven.

Monica: And there you are.

Rachel: (stretches arms above her head) Yeah, that'll work.

As I watch Chandler try to form words, eventually giving up as they all awkwardly leave the room, I gulp in a huge breath, and it all releases in the loudest laugh I think I've ever let out. And I continue my boisterous laughter until tears are running down my face and I can't even breathe.

I play the video over and over again, until I could probably quote the scene right along with the characters, loving every second of it.

This is how Seth got his Dom name, Seven? It couldn't be more perfectly fitting. It combines his love of TV show quotes and his wonderful sense of humor—not to mention the naughty inclination of what Monica was calling the seventh erogenous zone.

When I finally pull myself together, I click reply to his e-mail.

Oh. My. God.

I seriously don't think I've ever laughed so hard in my life. And I can't think of a better Dom name for you after watching that video. It all makes perfect sense.

Thanks, Seth. I needed that.

Twyla

I smile as I press Send, leaning back on my pillow. I can't help but picture Seth's handsome face, what he would look like quoting the scene from *Friends*. He's so funny and animated to begin with, so I can only imagine.

With nothing else to do, I'm overcome with a very unfamiliar feeling.

Boredom.

For years, all I've done is eat, sleep, and work. Any downtime at work or between work hours and falling asleep were filled with research on whatever project I was assigned. And since I promised Astrid I wouldn't go into my usual planning mode, I have no idea what to do with myself.

I could read another one of my sister's books. The first one left on a cliffhanger, and I'm pretty curious to see what happens next.

Nah. Laughing so hard over the past half hour has amped me up, gotten my endorphins and adrenaline pumping. I'm too hyper to settle down enough to concentrate on the story. Instead, I open my Internet browser. Biting my lip, my fingertips type Seth's full name into the search engine without my consent. But to my surprise, out of all the people named Seth Owens that comes up in the results, not one is mine.

Mine. I snort. If only.

I scroll through the image results, clicking through the many pages Google has to offer, but my Seth's face doesn't appear anywhere. I'm so confused. I mean, you'd think a child prodigy who then went to MIT at age thirteen would make some kind of news, right? But there's nothing. And wasn't he surprised when I told him I didn't have any social medias? Why would he get the same shocked look everyone else does if he doesn't have any either?

Maybe it's under his other name.

I type in Seven Owens, but again, nothing pulls up. Trying one last thing, I finally get some good results when I type in Seven Club Alias.

I click on the link to the Facebook profile, but unfortunately, everything is private except for the profile picture. It's dark, ominous-looking, and I click on it to make it bigger. The room he took it in must've been dimly lit, but I can make out the dark shadow of a black leather mask. It covers his whole head, almost like an executioner's hood. I shiver, closing the picture.

I click on the About tab, but it's also all set to private. I think about creating a Facebook profile just so I can friend request him, but I stop myself. What if Brandon were to somehow find it and be able to track me down? The thought makes me shudder, and I close out of the Internet. When I do, I see I have an e-mail waiting in my inbox from Seth.

Twyla,

I should have waited to show you the video in person then, because I would have loved to see you laugh. The few times I've gotten to witness your beautiful smile and laughter aren't nearly enough.

Do you have the day off tomorrow? I'm available if you'd like to have your next lesson. Roxy told me how well you did at the shop today. I'm one proud teacher.

Love,

Seth

Love, Seth. The signature makes butterflies erupt in my belly, making me feel silly. I'm sure he didn't mean anything by it, but it feels meaningful all the same. That combined with his other sweet words does funny things to other parts of my body as well. I respond immediately, my fingers seeming to have a mind of their own. But I decide to take a leap and just go with it.

Yes, sir! I had a great day at work today, thanks to the things you taught me. And I can't wait to learn more... and to spend time with you again. I don't have tomorrow off, but I don't go in until late. Should I come at the same time? 11 a.m.?
Love,
Twyla

His reply is almost immediate.

That would be perfect.
See you in the morning,
Seth
PS: Here's my phone number. Feel free to text me anytime. Ya know, if you have a question about anything at work. Or if you're bored or something.

I smile at the end of his e-mail. For someone so confident, with a presence so commanding, it almost sounded like he was pretty shy about trying to find a reason to give me his number. Instead of e-mailing him back, I decide to text him so he can have my phone number as well, after adding him to my contacts.

Me: I'm bored or something. And I don't like it. I've never been bored before, and now I get why you hear children sounding so distraught when they whine to their parents, "I'm booooored." It's a terrible feeling. Like I don't know what to do with my life.
Seth: LOL! I can picture you right now, squirming like Ricky Bobby. "I don't know what to do with my hands!"

Me: Is that another one of your TV show quotes?

Seth: Movie. Talladega Nights. Lord, woman. You kill me. But at the same time, it would be awesome to show you all my favorites and be able to see your reactions when you watch them for the first time.

My heart skips a beat. Was that an offer, or is he just making conversation? I don't want to make a fool of myself, so I just keep my response light.

Me: That would definitely help with the boredom.

Seth: Then it's a date. I have Sunday off. We're having a movie marathon at my place.

I read the text in the same demanding tone he used on me in the club and feel myself clench.

Me: Can't wait. Goodnight, Seth.

Seth: Night, doll.

I put my phone on the charger and make my way into the living room where Astrid is stretched out on one end of the sectional with her laptop. I plop down beside her, and adjust until my head is lying on her shoulder, watching silently as she answers questions about makeup in her private Facebook group.

"You okay, little sis?" she asks, finishing up a post about mixing a shade of lipstick with a different color of gloss to give it a unique effect.

"I'm bored. And I don't like it. I feel lost," I admit, and feel her rest her cheek on top of my head.

"I bet that is a pretty weird feeling for you. I've never seen you with downtime before." She giggles, and I frown to myself. "Anything exciting happen today?"

"Had a really good day at work. Sold a bunch of the things Seth taught me about." I pause, gearing myself up to speak aloud something I've never in my life said before. "And... I have a date. On Sunday."

"A date! With who?" she squeals, shimmying her shoulder to make me sit up and look at her.

"With Seth. He wants me to come over to watch movies at his place," I reply.

She gets a serious look on her face. "Oh, sweet Twy. That's code."

My brow furrows. "Code? For what?"

"When a guy asks you to come over to watch movies, it's code for getting you snuggled up in bed so a few minutes later he can get you naked. Have you never heard of 'Netflix and chill'?" she questions, and I give her a blank stare. "Right. Of course not. Just... be prepared, sis. Don't put yourself in the situation if you're not ready for it. And take your pepper spray just in case."

I nod. "Okay. But I don't think I'd need it. Not with Seth. He wouldn't pressure me into anything I don't want to do. He's... there's a gentleness to his soul," I tell her, feeling silly, but I don't know any other way to explain it.

Astrid wraps her arm around my shoulders, pulling me closer. "You have no idea how happy it makes me to see you interested in a guy. And I hope you're right. God knows I wish I'd find one with a gentle soul, as you put it. There was nothing gentle about...."

She doesn't finish what she was saying, but she doesn't need to. I know exactly what she was thinking. "You'll find someone else, big sis. Someone who'll never raise a hand to you and will treat you like a queen."

She snorts. "Pity."

I look into her sparkling blue eyes. "What?"

"A few years ago, when I first started reading the BDSM romances, I asked Brandon if we could try it. The sex had gotten kind of... boring, and I thought it would spice things up a bit. I only wanted to add a toy or something. Maybe a little spanking. But he got super offended. Tried to make it seem like I hurt his feelings, saying he wasn't good enough in bed anymore," she confessed.

I scoff. "Yeah right. That man had no feelings to hurt."

"You're right. And I know this because after the first time he hit me, he said I asked for it, and if I tried to tell anyone he hurt me, he'd just show them all my books and how I'd begged him to do it."

I wrap my arm across her stomach and squeeze her tight. We're silent for a while, as she answers a few messages and invoices some of her customers, signing each e-mail with her fake name, Roberta Card. When she'd decided on the name, she explained her favorite musician was Blackmill, a dubstep producer from Scotland whose real name is Robert Card. Spending so much time with her these past couple of months, and watching how serene she gets as she relaxes, listening to the melodic electronic songs, her choice made perfect sense. His music and her love of makeup both make my sister's soul happy, something she hadn't got to experience in a long time.

When she finishes and closes her laptop, we say goodnight and head to our bedrooms. I don't fall asleep right away, unable to stop thinking about seeing Seth tomorrow for my next lesson, and Sunday, wondering just what would happen when I'm alone with him at his place.

Surprisingly, it's not fear that my sister is right about what he really wants to do instead of actually watching movies. It's excitement. I mean, who better to lose your V-card to than a master of sex? He'd know exactly what to do to make it a good experience.

And it didn't hurt that my feelings for the handsome, hilarious, caring man were growing exponentially the more time I spent talking to him.

Six

Seth

"TELL ME WHAT YOU SEE BEFORE you, lovely Twyla," I quiz, pulling the rolling table in front of where she's seated in the leather chair against the wall of our playroom.

She sits up straight, looking over the different toys I've lined up neatly. "Waterproof vibrator. Butt plug. Umm... that sorta looks like an un-rolled-out condom, but there's nothing in the center of the ring. Aaand... yeah, that's all I've got," she lists, and I can't help but smile.

She said all of that without blushing once. She looks much more relaxed today than she did at our first lesson, and I feel accomplished knowing I've helped loosen her up around this stuff. Especially now that I know not only has she never used sex toys but has no sexual experience whatsoever.

I pick up one of the products she got wrong, holding it up in front of her face. "This is a cock ring. The primary purpose of wearing one is to restrict the flow of blood from an erect penis to create a stronger erection, or to maintain a hard-on for a longer period of time. For a guy, it creates sensations of tightness and pressure that many find pleasurable, and for a woman... well, let's just say if a guy has problems keeping it up, this'll make him last long enough to where she doesn't want to gut him for leaving her wanting."

She takes it out of my hand, rolling it onto three of her fingers before testing out how stretchy it is. She looks up at me curiously. "Have you ever tried one on before?"

"Yes," I answer, watching her eyes lower to the front of my pants as I feel my cock twitch in response.

"It seems like it would be really uncomfortable. Wouldn't it be bad to cut off your circulation down there? I mean, even a hair tie that's too tight around my wrist makes my hand all tingly, and not in a good way. Would it be the same for your, uh...."

She doesn't finish her question, but since I want to teach her to be more confident when it comes to this subject, the only way to do that is to force her to speak the words. "Would it be the same for my what, doll?"

I see her swallow, gathering her courage to ask her question. She meets my eyes. "Would it be the same for your, um, penis? Would it cut off the circulation?"

I give her a small smile in acknowledgment of her working past her shyness. "Newbies should avoid the ones with little to no stretch to them. The cock ring should never be in place for more than twenty minutes. And if any numbness, pain, or coldness occurs, the guy should discontinue use."

She nods. "Got it." She places the ring on the tray, warily eyeing the last two things I've set out.

"Today, I thought we'd have a male theme. Everything here can be sold to a man for his pleasure. Ladies aren't the only ones who come into the store looking for a little something extra in the bedroom," I tell her, watching her eyes widen as they go from the tray of toys, up to me, and then back down to the tray again before biting her lip. "You got the butt plug right."

"How could I ever forget what one of those looks like?" she murmurs, scrunching up her face.

I chuckle, pushing her hair back behind her ear, and my stomach does something funny when she leans into my touch. "Nah, I guess you wouldn't, huh?"

She smiles up at me then, and something passes between us I can't explain. Time seems to stand still, and everything around us disappears. The only thing I see is the marbling inside her blue irises. She looks at me so trustingly, with such admiration. Like she's hanging on to my every word. This may not be her favorite subject, but it feels almost like she'd be willing to learn just about anything as long as I was the one teaching her.

I can feel her eyes begging me to lean closer, to close the distance between us and kiss her. And God, how I want to. I've never wanted to kiss a woman so badly in my life, and not to lead to anything more, but to just feel her lips pressed against mine while I breathe her in.

A vision of our first lesson flashes through my mind.

"I'm a virgin," she said, and she visibly held her breath, waiting for my reaction.

Stone-faced on the outside, I acted like she'd just told me nothing more than the weather forecast for the day, when inside I felt like she'd smacked me upside the head, with little Tweety Birds flying around in a circle around me.

"I see. Well then, no. You probably wouldn't want to try out the Wild Orchid." My voice was completely calm. "Okay, doll. This changes things."

Her voice came out small, and I wanted to punch myself for making her feel anything less than the perfection she is. "Does... does that mean you won't teach me anymore?"

"No!" I exclaimed, making her jump a little. "No, Twyla. I'll still teach you. It just means I'll have to explain things in more detail because you haven't experienced the sensations and stuff a lot of the toys I'm teaching you about provide."

She let out a sigh of relief.

"But it also means I need to ask you more questions about yourself. I need to know what you have done before so I can figure out a way to help you better understand the products." It wasn't a lie. I really did need to know her actual experience level in order to know where to start. But I also wanted to know for myself. What would it be like to be Twyla's first?

"Well, I haven't done anything, pretty much," she replied.

"You are a virgin, but... let's work our way backward from sex. Have you given or received oral?"

No hesitation. "No."

"Given a hand job, been fingered?"

Her cheeks pinken. "No."

"Made out with anyone with heavy petting? Breast play?"

She shifted her weight from foot to foot where she stood between my legs as I sat on the padded table inside the playroom. "No, none of that."

My voice came out deep and soft with my last question, my

cock straining against the zipper of my jeans. "Have you never been kissed, Twyla?"

She looked up into my eyes, searching but finding no judgment there, so she whispered, "Not properly."

In this moment, I'd do just about anything to be the one to give Twyla her first proper kiss. But not here. Not when I know she's never been with anyone before. I don't want her first real kiss to be next to a tray of anal sex toys in the middle of one of my club's playrooms. She deserves more than that.

So instead of leaning down as her eyes implore, as everything inside me commands, I slide my finger up the bridge of her little nose to push her glasses back into place before gently tapping the tip of it. I try without speaking to make her understand I'm not rejecting her, and she seems to get it, because her face softens and she gives me a secret smile.

She's the one to break the silence. "So um... that one's kind of terrifying. What's it for?" She nudges her chin toward the last toy on the tray.

"Ah, sweet Twyla." I grin wickedly as I pick it up and hand it to her. "That's a vibrating, ribbed anal probe."

And I don't think I've ever laughed harder than when I see her toss the toy back onto the tray like it's a snake about to bite her.

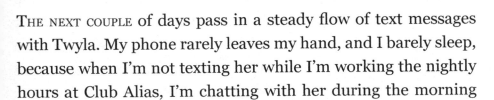

THE NEXT COUPLE of days pass in a steady flow of text messages with Twyla. My phone rarely leaves my hand, and I barely sleep, because when I'm not texting her while I'm working the nightly hours at Club Alias, I'm chatting with her during the morning while she's at work, when I'd normally be dead to the world. That, and I have no appetite for the buffet of submissives at the club since meeting her, so no time is killed in the playrooms either.

Every spare minute, I'm talking with Twyla, learning more and more about her. Her likes and dislikes. Her favorite music, which she knows much more about than TV shows and movies, because she said she always had her radio playing in her lab at work in California.

I haven't learned the reason why she and her sister decided to move here, especially considering she'd been a rising star in her industry back home; the subject somehow always changes before we delve too deeply. But she did tell me all about her loving parents. Her mom was a homemaker, and her dad ran his own car detailing business, which apparently brought in a ton of money with the caliber of cars in the area they lived in California, somewhere between LA and San Diego. They sold their large family home on the West Coast once both of their daughters graduated high school, and then moved to Florida to retire. They made sure their girls were set up in college first, but having been in their late thirties when they'd had Astrid then forty when they had Twyla, all of them agreed the move to the slower-paced and relaxed community of Orange Tree, Florida would be wonderful for them.

I asked Twyla why she and her sister hadn't moved near her parents if they were just looking for a change, but a customer had arrived at the shop. When she texted me back, it was to tell me what she'd sold, and we never went back to the original question.

I might not know what brought the raven-haired beauty to our small town, but whatever it was, I become more and more grateful for it with every passing hour I spend getting to know her. It feels like I've known her for so much longer than the week that's passed, and more than that, I trust her. I've told her more about myself than any female on the planet. Only Doc, Corbin, and Bryan know me better, and that's only because of the years we've spent together, more as brothers than just partners. That, and our mercenary business.

What would she think if she found out we kill people for paychecks? Whether we have a code or not, not every girl in the world would be as cool with the fact we take people's lives as Corbin's wife, Vi, was. She'd barely batted an eyelash, but she'd been a military wife to begin with, used to the thought of her husband killing bad guys. Sweet Twyla, though—so innocent, so sheltered by her own introverted personality—never having been around such violence, how would she react?

But there was no need for me to worry about it since we hadn't even shared our first kiss yet. I was getting way ahead of myself.

Yet the fact I was even thinking about it told me she was more special than anyone I'd ever met.

Seven

Twyla

SUNDAY MORNING, I LEAVE THE convenience store loaded down with tons of snacks. French onion dip, wavy potato chips, Reese's Peanut Butter Cups, Cheetos, pretzel chips, and hummus fill the plastic bags on my arm as I text Seth, letting him know I'm on my way.

The store is just a couple of blocks from my apartment, which is within walking distance of Club Alias, so I didn't bother driving. I was so anxious about our date anyway that I figured the exercise would do me good, hoping it would expend some of my jitters.

I smile at his incoming message.

Seth: Guardians of the Galaxy is all loaded! Can't wait for you to get here.

I slip my phone into my back pocket and hurry my pace.

Suddenly, a weird feeling comes over me, like I'm being watched. I glance up the street, seeing that most of the stores are closed since it's Sunday. The only thing open is the little café up ahead on the left, but I don't notice anyone looking my way. I peek over my shoulder, but no one is there. There are a couple of cars parked along the curb, but I don't stop to search if there's anyone in them.

Trying to shake off the eerie feeling, I quicken my steps, spotting the club up ahead. *Maybe it's just Seth watching me from a window or something*, I think. But by the time I reach the unmarked door, I'm so freaked out that I yank it open and take the stairs two at a time. When I reach the very top, I turn to look down the steps to make sure no one followed me inside, completely shaken even when I see no one's there.

As I turn to make my way toward the staircase to my right, I run straight into a tall, hard body and let out a scream that echoes around the empty club. Arms like steel band around me, and it's not until I smell the familiar scent of leather and Seth that I stop fighting and cut off my shriek of terror.

"Shhhh, hey, hey, beautiful. What's wrong?" His deep, soothing voice washes over me, and I drop the plastic bags to the floor and immediately wrap my arms around his waist, my heart pounding hard in my chest. "Twyla, you're shaking. What happened?"

I relax against him, my head resting on his chest, listening to the steady thrum of his heart as mine slows to match its beat. It's then I realize our position. I've never been so close to a man before, our fronts pressed tightly together without the slightest space for even air to pass between us. I close my eyes, memorizing the feel of his muscular arms around me as his hands slide up and down my back. The heat of him soaks into me, doing even more to erase my fright.

I lose track of time. I have no idea how long he allows me to stay like that, cocooned by his strong, towering body, feeling like nothing bad could ever reach me as long as I stay right here in his wonderful embrace. But finally, he takes hold of my shoulders and leans slightly away to look down into my face.

"You all right, doll?" he asks gently.

"I am now," I breathe.

"What happened?" he tries again, and this time, I have my wits enough to reply.

"I had the strangest feeling, like I was being followed."

His brow furrows. "Did you see anyone?"

I shake my head. "No, but I was too scared to turn around and take a good look. It was probably nothing."

"If it makes you feel any better, this is a pretty safe little town, Twyla. Nothing like what you're probably used to in California," he tells me reassuringly, and I relax even more. "Do you know of anyone who would be following you? You don't have any stalker ex-boyfriends I've gotta worry about, do I? Because I will fuck them up."

He grins, trying to make me laugh, but his question hits too close to home. I *do* know someone who could be looking for my sister. But I don't want Seth to know about any of that. I'd rather Astrid and I just move on with our lives and forget about her abusive ex. Surely after two and a half months he would have given up finding her anyway.

I force a smile, but he sees right through it. "Would it make you feel better if I lock the front door?" When I nod, he traces the line of my jaw, sending tingles down my neck. "One sec, doll."

I watch as he gallops down the stairs, his light brown hair disappearing from sight for a moment as I hear him lock the glass door in the otherwise completely silent club before he returns.

"There. You ready to watch the awesomeness that is a Marvel movie now?" he asks, kneeling to gather up all the snacks I'd dropped. "French onion dip? My favorite!"

The pure joy on his face erases any lingering feelings of unease I have, replacing it with delight that this sexy-ass, delicious man could get so excited over chips and dip. "Yes. I'm ready to see this Star Lord guy. Apparently he's super hot, according to my sister."

"Not as hot as me, but he ain't ugly." He wiggles his eyebrows.

I let out a girlish giggle, placing my hand in his when he reaches out to take it. "I believe you," I say, biting my lip.

He looks surprised at my admission, and his grin widens before he leads me up the stairs. He opens the door at the top, and we enter a long hallway, passing by four offices, two on each side, before it ends at another door, this one with a keypad on the wall beside it. He types in a code and I hear a loud click, which must be the lock mechanism opening. He turns the knob and pushes the door open, pulling me inside.

When it closes again, I hear the same loud click and realize I'm now locked inside Seth's loft with no way to escape if I wanted to. I wait for a feeling of unease to come over me, but it never does. Instead, I feel completely safe, like nothing bad could happen to me as long as I'm here with him.

I look around the place, trying to gain insight into the man who owns it. It's nothing like I imagined it. I'm so used to seeing Seth surrounded by black leather and deep, blood-red in dim, sexy lighting. I never thought his home would be all bright colors and brilliant light.

His loft is one large open space, with two doors against the far-left wall. That must be the bathroom and a closet, because to my right is the kitchen. In front of it is the living area, and to the left of that is his huge, king-size bed. On the wall between the two doors is a computer the likes I've never seen before, with six massive screens and equipment I couldn't tell you what it was for. No surprise a technology prodigy who graduated with his masters from MIT would have a setup like this.

His bed is pure white, aside from the tall, light-brown headboard that looks like the wood has been woven together. The white down comforter looks so fluffy and soft I want to run and jump on top of it to feel myself sink into its depths.

I glance to my right as Seth pulls out the snacks and spreads them over the marble countertop. The cabinets are a pale gray and his refrigerator, stove, and dishwasher are all stainless steel, but all the small appliances and cooking utensils are bright green. Even his dishtowels and the few plates resting in the drying rack next to the sink have a green pattern along the edges. Butted up against the kitchen island is the most comfortable-looking couch I've ever seen. The cushions look like they would swallow me whole. The upholstery is topped with several throw pillows in a mix of greens and blues. There's a coffee table in front of it, and what looks to be a half wall separating the space from the bedroom area, but standing on this side of it, you can clearly see the entire loft, the walls all painted the color of a sandy beach.

Seth walks around the kitchen island, a roll of paper towels beneath one bicep, his hands full with two plates, and the bag of potato chips clenched between his teeth. He places everything on the coffee table, and then falls backward onto the couch, patting the cushion next to him as he smiles up at me, where I'm still standing just inside the door.

Suddenly, my sister's warning pops into my head. Am I ready for whatever Seth has planned for today, if she's right about "watching a movie" being code for sex? Surprisingly, the idea doesn't terrify me. After the two lessons we've had, and now recognizing how safe I feel when I'm with him, I realize I won't stop him if he wants to get physical.

I take a seat beside him, looking around, confused.

"Um, Seth? Where's the TV?" I ask, wondering how we're supposed to even pretend to watch the movie.

He pops a dip-covered chip into his mouth before grabbing a remote off the coffee table, then turns to watch my reaction when he pushes a button. Out of the corner of my eye, I see something move, and when I face forward, I see a giant flat-screen TV rising from the half wall.

"Holy crap! That's cool!" I gush, watching as it finally stops growing only an inch from the ceiling.

He pushes a few more buttons, and I'm completely mesmerized as blinds cover all the windows along the top of the loft, the lights dim overhead, and the menu for *Guardians of the Galaxy* fills the TV screen. He clicks one last button before setting the remote back down on the coffee table, and the movie begins.

As Seth powers through his chips, dip, and pizza, which I see he's also put on the plate in front of me, I sit quietly, laughing at the few parts of the movie I'm able to concentrate on. The rest of the time, I'm only aware of my heart trying to beat its way out of my chest, along with the heat at the right side of my body, where

Seth's thigh presses against mine. I'm too nervous to eat, and when he glances down at my plate to find I haven't touched a single bit of the food there, he grabs a paper towel from the roll, wipes his hands and his mouth, and then turns to face me.

"You okay, doll? You aren't still shook up from earlier, are you? Because I can promise you, nothing can get you in here. It's a fucking fortress," he assures, his voice confident.

I shake my head then slide my glasses back up my nose. "No, I'm good," I fib, staring at the screen, but not seeing anything playing across it. My mind is elsewhere, specifically on the man next to me. I'm hyperaware of his closeness, his intoxicating scent, the roughness of his jeans against my bare leg. I'd worn my stretch workout shorts and a tank with my hoodie since he told me to dress comfortably for our all-day movie marathon.

I feel his fingers at my chin as he turns me to face him, discovering disappointment in his gaze. It's like a punch to my gut.

"On day one, we promised each other to be completely open and honest, Twyla. And I know you're not being truthful with me right now. What's the matter?"

I can't handle him looking at me like that. And that tone... that gently commanding tone that leaves no room for denial. My walls crumble.

"I'm having a hard time relaxing, it seems. My um... my sister told me that when a guy invites a chick over to watch a movie, they don't actually want to... uh... watch a movie. And since this is my first time on a date, I don't really know what... I don't know what to do with my hands." I use the quote he'd texted me, trying for humor as I hold my hands up in front of me and wiggle my fingers.

He studies me closely, his beautiful eyes searching my face. I put my hands back down in my lap when he doesn't smile, just keeps hunting for something in my expression until I grow self-conscious and can't meet his stare any longer. My eyes lower to where our legs are pressed together, and while he continues either playing connect the dots with my freckles inside his head or picking apart what I said, I admire how different our thighs are. Mine is lightly tan and lean, not a hair in sight because after what Astrid said, I'd taken great care shaving my legs this morning. His is covered with dark denim, but it's so thick with strength I can see the dips and bulges of the muscle beneath the fabric.

Finally, he speaks. "Twyla, are you telling me you came here thinking we were going to make love?"

I swallow past the lump in my throat, my mouth suddenly as dry as the desert I drove through two and a half months ago. I can feel him still searching my face. I'd promised him complete honesty, and I always keep my promises. I meet his breathtaking eyes.

"I came here thinking that if she was right, then I wouldn't object." My answer hangs in the air between us like a physical thing as I wait for him to respond.

"First, let me start out by saying if that's what I was inviting you over for, then I would have just said so. I am a Dom. I do not have to hide what I want behind sayings such as 'Netflix and chill' like pussies who are too afraid to state what they actually mean." Even though his words are almost scolding, like I'm in trouble with my teacher and being sent to the principal's office, there's a hint of warmth mixed with that commanding tone of his that keeps me entranced rather than flinching away. "I asked you over, honestly, for us to just watch movies all day. This in itself is a big deal. You are the first woman I have ever wanted to spend all day doing nothing but veg out with. You are also the only woman I have ever invited into my personal space. No one besides my business partners and myself has ever stepped foot inside this apartment."

I gasp, my eyes widening at his admission. The hint of warmth in his voice sparks an inferno inside me, and I have to fight for control, as my body wants to do nothing but melt right here in this spot.

He reaches up, tracing along my jawline before his hand rests at the side of my neck as he continues, "At most, I thought—if I was lucky—you might curl up with me here on my couch. And, if I was even luckier, we might end the night with me giving you your very first kiss. I was looking forward to a day of firsts, but never once did I expect to fill the day with *all* your firsts, doll."

I bite my lip. I have no idea how to respond to that.

"But yet you came here believing we might. And you said you wouldn't object if that's what I really wanted you here for." A pause. "You want me to be your first, Twyla? You want to give me that honor?"

My heart pounds in my chest. If I say yes, what will happen? Will he cut off the movie, carry me to his huge white bed, and make love to me as soon as the word leaves my lips? Am I prepared for that to happen if I give him my answer, that yes, I want him to be the one to take my virginity?

With nothing else to do but give him my honesty like I swore I would do, I bravely meet his eyes and whisper, "Yes, Seth."

His grip on the side of my neck tightens, making my lids slide to half-mast and my core clench. He uses that grip to pull me forward until I'm pressed against the hard planes of his chest.

"Lovely Twyla. My beautiful doll." His other hand wraps around the small of my back, and he pulls me onto his lap, almost cradling me in his big, strong arms. "Today, you can relax. We'll watch our movies, eat junk food, and spend our time laughing. Another day, though, I'll take you to my bed, and you'll spend the time screaming my name while I make you come."

My whole body shudders at his wicked words. I grow instantly slick between my legs, feeling his hardness beneath me. He's going to make me wait. How I went from nervous about the possibility of it happening to completely disappointed it's not going to right now, I have no idea. But as he denies me for the time being, it makes me realize without a shadow of a doubt that I want him. I want this amazing, smart, beautiful, protective, caring, and patient man to be my first.

Without thinking, my eyes close and I lean forward, ready to take my first kiss. But that firm hand at the side of my neck stops my movement, and my eyelids spring open. What I find when my gaze meets his... I'm not sure how to describe it. Confusion? He looks like he's fighting something within himself. I don't understand. But then his hold relaxes, allowing me to slowly close the space between us, and I see his eyes close just as my lips meet his and mine do the same.

Seth

It's been a long time since I've kissed a woman.

The act is so intimate, more affectionate than what I'm normally willing to give to a submissive in my club. No, there's usually very little skin-to-skin contact when I act out a scene in a playroom. I use a wide variety of toys and devices on them for foreplay, but I never get undressed, always wear my hooded mask, and rarely ever stroke their flesh with my hands. Then after that, it's only my condom-covered cock that receives any pleasure.

Already, I've touched more of Twyla than any submissive. I can't seem to stop myself from toying with her hair, sliding my finger down the bridge of her upturned nose, or stroking the delicate line of her jaw every chance I get. I held her trembling body when she first arrived, feeling her fear seep away as I rubbed her back, breathing in the scent of her dark hair. Even the innocent press of her leg against mine while we sat side by side watching the movie gave me more of a thrill than what a full-on

BDSM scene has in quite some time.

And then I pulled her into my lap, feeling the heat of her atop my throbbing erection, with her face so very close to mine. It was all I could do not to come in my pants right there when she leaned forward to take her first kiss. Especially after she'd just told me she wants to give me her virginity. My grip on her delicate neck had tightened while I tried to gain control of myself, confused by how the woman in my arms had so much power over me. She's taken over my every thought, my every spare moment, and now, apparently, my control over my own body.

When I finally feel like I can handle it without exploding like a twelve-year-old boy, I relax my arm and allow her to close the short distance between our mouths. Tentative at first, her lips gently press against mine, and we both gasp as a wave of pure bliss and belonging fills me.

That's when I snap. My hand at her neck dives in to the back of her thick, shoulder-length hair where I grasp the back of her skull as I deepen the kiss. All plans I'd had to let her control her first kiss, to let her explore me the way she wanted to, goes right out the window. When she moans at my forcefulness, my tongue slides between her soft, pillowy lips to dance with hers. She's hesitant at first, not knowing what to do, but soon, she's mimicking my movements, and we lose ourselves in the passion of the moment.

It may be her very first kiss, but it's the very *best* kiss I've ever had in my life. It's like our movements are choreographed. We just fit together so perfectly, and she tastes so goddamn good. And if just kissing her feels this fucking amazing, I can only imagine what being inside her will feel like.

I don't know how long we stay like that, her in my lap, making out like a couple of teenagers, but soon enough, it enters my consciousness that the movie's menu has been playing the same song clip over and over and over. As much as I'd love to throw out what I told Twyla about just relaxing today and making her mine another day, I can't. I want to wait. I don't want to rush everything. I just found her, and I want each of our milestones to mean something. I want our special moments to get the spotlight they deserve. For the first time, I want to be one of those annoying couples who have a hundred different anniversaries they look forward to each year. The day they met, the first date, the first kiss, the day they officially became a couple, the first time they made love... the little yet important anniversaries leading up to all the big ones everyone else mildly cares about.

For the rest of the day, we alternate watching my favorite episodes of TV shows, movies, and making out. When it grows dark, I walk her home, laughing when I realize she lives in Vi's old apartment. She invites me in to meet her sister, and I tell them all about the romance novelist married to my best friend and partner. Astrid immediately downloads all the books written under the pen name VB Lowe onto her Kindle, and as I kiss Twlya goodnight, I inform her Vi got all her information about BDSM from me. Seeing the spark of interest in her eyes, I tell her goodbye with a cocky smirk, knowing what she'll spend the rest of her night doing.

Eight

Twyla

MAYBE IT WAS THE FACT I WAS STILL floating on a cloud after my date with Seth.

Maybe it was because I got very little sleep last night, as I stayed up devouring one of the books his friend Vi wrote, knowing Seth was the one who taught her everything she'd put in the stories. Not to mention the long phone conversation we had in the middle of the night, where he basically decided on his own that sometime next week we'd be going away to some beach house one of his partners owns. When I reminded him I have to work, he told me not to worry about it; he'd have a talk with my boss. He used his bossy voice, so there was no arguing.

Or maybe it was because he'd made me feel completely safe for the first time in almost three months, allowing me to let my guard down and just be in the moment.

Whatever the reason may have been, as I came upon my car in the underground garage of my apartment building the next morning, after spending so many hours thinking about nothing but Seth and the way he makes me feel whole, it doesn't even register what I'm looking at.

I pick up the envelope that's held down to the glass by my windshield wiper, turning it over in my hand. Scrawled across the front in red is the name Roberta Card. Is this one of my sister's makeup statements? If so, why would they put it on my car? Plus, there's no mailing label on the outside, just the name. No one here knows my sister's online persona. Hell, no one besides me *anywhere* knows that Roberta Card is actually Astrid Quill.

A terrible feeling washes over me, turning my insides to bricks of ice, and I shiver. What do I do? God only knows what's inside the envelope. I've studied enough shit to remember the different chemicals sent through the mail to hurt people when a letter is opened. Agent Orange, anyone?

One thing is for certain: I don't want to tell Astrid. She's been through enough. If I can take care of this without her ever finding out, that would be the best course of action.

My first instinct is to run to Seth, into his arms, my safe place. I'd give anything to just go to him and hide in his fortress of an apartment, and just pretend I didn't find some creepy envelope on my car, with a name on it that no one should know. But I just found him. Our relationship, if I can even call it that yet, is so new. I don't want to suddenly drop this bomb on him.

Or I could be completely overreacting, and it's something the mailman dropped off, matching the name to the various shipments of makeup my sister receives. But the mailman wouldn't know my car. And wouldn't he just leave it at the front office?

No, I know something is wrong. This isn't some innocent piece of mail. I can feel it. So what do I do? Do I go to the police? No, can't do that either. I don't want to draw any attention to us. In such a small town, I'm sure word spreads fast when police get involved with anything.

Something niggles at my mind. A security office. Didn't I see one next to Club Alias? I'm not exactly sure what they could do, but maybe they'll at least have some advice.

I hop in my car, too creeped out to walk the short distance after this, and from the weird feeling of being watched yesterday. I pull up in front of Imperium Security only a couple minutes later, texting Roxanne that I may be a little late for my shift before grabbing the letter off my passenger seat. The business hours on the door show they just opened, so hopefully there won't be anyone ahead of me.

I pull open the glass door, the electronic bell dinging as I enter the empty room. And as the door behind the front desk opens, my brow furrows as Seth walks out.

"Well hello there, doll," he greets, coming around the desk to pull me against him.

I glance behind me stupidly, making sure I hadn't gone through the unmarked entrance of Club Alias by mistake before turning to meet his smiling face once again. "What are you doing here?" I ask, wondering if he's just visiting his business neighbor.

"I could ask you the same thing, but since you asked first... I work here," he replies with a shrug.

"But I thought this was a security office. Like... an office... with um, security guards or something." I'm so confused.

"Let's just call this my day job," he states, before letting go of me to take a seat in the rolling chair behind the desk. "And what might you need from an office with security guards or something, lovely Twyla?"

I bite my lip, wondering if I should tuck tail and run. I hadn't gone to Seth because I wasn't ready to explain the darkness of my sister's past, which had brought us to the other side of the country. Anytime he asked me about why I left California, I always changed the subject. But now, do I really have a choice? My promise to always be open and honest tells me no.

I slump in defeat and take the seat in front of him, placing the envelope on top of the desk. "This was on my car this morning. I don't know who it's from, and whoever it is shouldn't have that name."

He picks up the envelope, flipping it over to see I haven't opened it yet. "Who's Roberta Card?"

I take a deep breath. "My sister, Astrid. That's the fake name she uses for her online makeup business."

"I see." He sits back in his chair and meets my eyes. "Are you finally ready to tell me what brought you two here? What are you running from?"

I gulp down the lump in my throat and then begin. "My older sister was in an abusive relationship. He'd always been terribly controlling, but then the emotional abuse turned physical." His brow furrows and he sits forward, taking my hand when my voice cracks. "You wondered why a successful chemical engineer is now working somewhere she hasn't the foggiest idea what she's doing? It's because I quit my job and basically rescued Astrid from her own home. She snuck out in the middle of the night, and we drove across the country, not knowing where the hell we were going, just that we wanted it to be far, far away from him. This is where fate landed us."

"And you said this name, Roberta Card, is a fake name she made up for her online business?"

"Yes. She makes pretty good money selling makeup in a Facebook group. When we moved, she posted that she was quitting so Brandon wouldn't be able to see her activity, but then private messaged each of her customers and referred them to Roberta Card so she could delete her old profile," I explain.

"No one else knows that name? Just her online customers?" he questions.

I shake my head. "No one. And none of them would know where she lives now."

He holds the envelope up to the light, trying to see what's inside it before lowering it back to the desk. "It seems to only be paper inside. Do you want me to open it?"

I look down in my lap. "I'm sorry, Seth. I didn't mean to get you involved in all this," I murmur.

"Twyla," he says in his commanding tone, and my eyes lift to his. "My only regret is you didn't come straight to *me*, knowingly. I know it's happening a little fast, this thing between us, but I want to be the person you turn to when you're afraid, when you need anything. I want to be involved in your everything, even the bad parts."

My eyes fill with tears, so unused to anyone wanting to be close to me, much less wanting to be the person I run to. I nod vigorously, wiping the corners of my eyes. "I want that too," I confess, and feel him squeeze my hand before letting go.

He opens the drawer in front of him and pulls out a silver letter opener, and a pair of rubber gloves from the one beside him. He slips them on, and then carefully slices the top of the legal-size envelope, sliding a personal-size one out that had already been ripped open. Turning that one over in his hands, he then removes the folded sheet of paper inside.

I exhale the breath I didn't realize I was holding, seeing that's the only thing hidden inside. "What's it say?" I whisper, too nervous to speak any louder. My gut is still telling me it's something bad. After looking at the paper, he hands it over to me, and I read, my heart dropping solidly into my stomach.

Astrid Quill
372 Piney View Rd.
San Diego, CA 92106
Dear Tiara Beauty Consultant,
This is to confirm that your online shop's name has successfully been updated in our system.
Roberta Card
We see you've filled out a change of address form, which will take effect in 3-5 business days. New shipments of products will be sent after this address has been confirmed, so please look for that letter's arrival at the new address.
We appreciate your business,
Your friends at Tiara Beauty

I glance up at Seth, my hand trembling as I grip the letter. "But—" My voice cracks, so I clear my throat and try again. "But he couldn't find her just by a name, right? She has a post office box for her business, not a real home address."

I can't read his face as he wiggles the mouse on the desk, bringing his computer to life. And as he turns the wide screen to face me more, I watch with growing horror as he begins his search.

He types into Google: *Roberta Card.*

The first link in the search results: www.tiarabeauty.com/RobertaCard

He clicks on the link, and on the left is a menu. The first option: Meet Your Consultant.

We read Astrid's fake profile, and at the bottom, the payment options she accepts. Visa, MasterCard, American Express, and PayPal.

He goes back to Google and types in *Roberta Card Tiara Beauty PayPal.*

And I choke back a sob when in the summary below the first search result is the new town we live in.

That fast.

That fast, and Seth already showed me how easy it would be for Brandon to find Astrid just by knowing her new fake name. He didn't even have to break out his technical genius skills. Just a simple Google search and the monster we've been hiding from narrowed us down to the small blip on the map where we've been living.

"Anyone could've found that, doll. And if he hired anyone to dig further...." He begins typing, and an array of screens flash before my eyes. He works so quickly I barely have time to register the words *IP Address Location* before a map of Earth fills the screen. It feels as if my heart stops beating as it zooms in until I'm staring at my apartment building.

I feel dizzy, and before I even know what's happening, I see Seth lunge at me. And everything goes black.

"...FREAKING OUT SAYING she felt like she was being watched yesterday, and now this. What should we do, Doc?"

I hear Seth's voice as if he's at a far distance. Did he say Doc? Where am I? A hospital? I can't seem to open my eyes to see what's going on.

"Looks like your little doll is starting to come around," a deep, masculine voice says, confusing me even more. Why would a doctor know the nickname Seth calls me? And in my jumbled thoughts, I realize I forgot to Google what he said about my name being linked to some kind of doll.

"Twyla? Hey, beautiful." I feel the stroke of his finger down my cheek, a smile pulling at the corners of my lips. I love it when he does that. "Open those pretty eyes for me."

I struggle and finally blink my eyes open, my lashes fluttering as I try to adjust to the bright light of the room we're in. My glasses are gently slid onto my face, and when I'm eventually able to focus, I see we're in one of the offices we passed yesterday when we were walking down the hallway toward Seth's loft, and I'm sprawled on a black leather couch. Seth's handsome face appears clearly right above me, and when I look over his shoulder, a ridiculously tall and handsome man with a goatee peers down at me with soft eyes.

"What happened?" I croak, trying to sit up.

"Whoa, baby. Chillax for a bit, okay? You fainted in our security office," Seth reminds me, and I nod, the movement making my head swim.

And then what we found registers in my confused brain.

"Oh, God. Oh, shit! Seth. He knows where we live! What if...." Something hits me. "She's there by herself. Seth, Astrid is home alone right now. And he left that letter on my car!" My voice is full of panic, but he stays calm, running his fingers through my hair.

"It's okay. We called her, and Doc was just about to leave to go pick her up when you started coming to," he tells me quietly.

"How did you call her? How do you know her number? It's brand-new. Could he have that—"

"Child prodigy. Masters from MIT, remember, doll?" He smiles, leaning down to kiss my forehead.

I look over his shoulder at the tall man. "You're Doc?"

"I am," he replies with a nod.

"What are you waiting for? Go get my sister. Please! You have no idea how horrible her ex is. He already turned her black and blue. I can't even imagine what he'd do now since she ran away from him." I don't mean to sound so rude. I just have a really bad feeling that I need to get her out of there and fast. "I'm sorry. I—"

"No need to apologize. I'll be right back with your sister. You just take it easy," he instructs as he leaves, and there's something in his voice that makes me do just that. He sounds very sure of himself, like what he says is fact. And the sheer size of him makes me believe that if he were to come face-to-face with Brandon, he'd be able to squash him like a bug.

"Don't worry, Twyla," Seth tells me. "We'll take care of it."

My eyes well up at the sincerity in his. "I'm so sorry. I never wanted you to have to know about this. I didn't want to be the girl with all the baggage. We just wanted a fresh start."

"We all have baggage, doll. And if you ask me, I consider myself lucky. Just call me Lucky Number Seven." He grins as he continues to stroke my hair.

"Why in the world would you consider yourself lucky having

to deal with a chick's sister's crazy ex?" My voice is squeaky with bewilderment.

"It's like what the brilliant Cher Horowitz once said. 'You see how picky I am about my shoes, and they only go on my feet,'" he says in a high-pitched voice mimicking a Valley girl. When he reads my blank face, his eyes turn up to the ceiling as he sighs. "What am I gonna do with you, woman? Cher Horowitz. *Clueless?*"

I shake my head, my face scrunching up.

"Dear God. Okay. Cher is the most beautiful, popular girl in school, and she's a virgin. Her new friend who moves to California from New York is scandalized by the fact she's never had sex before. Cher, and I quote, is 'saving herself for Luke Perry.' Meaning she's waiting for the right person." He leans down and kisses me softly on the lips before pulling back to whisper, "You chose me as your Luke Perry. I'm one lucky motherfucker. And if all I have to do is take care of one measly asshole stalking your sister, then that's something I am more than willing to do. Believe me, this is child's play compared to what we usually do in our line of work."

My face softens at his ability to turn a silly movie quote into something sweet and meaningful. And completely distracting.

"This makes much more sense," I tell him, and it's his turn to look confused. "A prodigal child, master in computers, who now owns a BDSM club... and runs a security company by day."

"Had to put my degree to use somehow, doll." He smirks, pretending to flip hair over his shoulder, and I can't help but giggle. "There's my smile." He traces my jawline with his fingertip. "Everything's gonna be all right, Twyla. We've got this. I promise."

I let myself sink back into the couch at his words, but still feel uneasy with my sister out of my sight. "I won't be able to completely relax until Astrid is here. Will you just talk to me until then? Tell me about Imperium Security. I definitely wasn't expecting to see you there." He stiffens a bit at my request, which is surprising. He's never had a problem answering any of my questions before. "Or not," I murmur, pulling his eyes back to me.

"No... it's not... I..." He sighs, all traces of his ever-present humor disappearing. His face turns serious, putting me on edge. This isn't the reaction I was anticipating. "I made a promise to you. I swore that if you were open and honest with me, then I would do the same." He pauses a moment, seeming to think carefully about his next words. "In light of the fact you were not ready for me to know everything about your past and didn't tell me the reason you moved here with your sister, I'd appreciate a pass on getting into the details of my security company... for right now."

I'm taken aback by this. On the one hand, he's actually being open and honest by revealing there is something he isn't ready to tell me about, and he has a point. It's only fair since I kept him in the dark about Brandon. Yet, on the other hand, his admission makes me ridiculously curious. But he did say it was just for now. I'd much rather he tell me when he's ready, seeing how he hadn't pressured me in any way when I avoided his questions about my recent past.

I smile gently, hoping to lower the drawbridge he'd yanked up inside himself at my question. "Pass granted."

He nods. "I'll tell you all about it sometime, doll. But for now, I'll give you this much. Our security team came first. It's run by me and my same partners here at the club. I was a little nervous about income, if we'd be able to make enough money in that line of work, so I opened up Club Alias. Imperium is the intellectual side of me. Club Alias is my passion. At least... I thought it was." His face goes from serious to mischievous.

My brow furrows. "What do you mean?"

His smile is heart stopping. "I thought what I felt when I'm in my Dom persona, when I'm Seven, was passion. But it doesn't compare in the slightest to what I feel when all I do is touch you." He slides his fingertip lightly down my nose and his eyes heat. "*That*... is passion."

If it weren't for being stuck to his leather couch, I would've slid right off onto the floor in a melted pile of goo. I had never dreamed of a man thinking about me in such a way, much less him being vocal about it.

I have no idea how to respond to that, and before I make a fool of myself even trying, we hear the door to the second-floor hallway open and then close with a heavy thud. Next thing I know, my sister is smothering me as she throws herself practically on top of me.

"Oh my God! Twy, what happened? That bullheaded giant wouldn't tell me anything except you fainted. Are you all right?" she frets, squeezing the life out of me.

I look up at Doc, and he reaches his hand up to run it down his face as he sighs. Clearly, she'd been a handful on the short drive over here from our apartment. I open my lips to answer her, but her long hair fills my mouth, and I sputter and wiggle to get her off me.

"Let's give her some air," Seth says, and Astrid sits up abruptly, her face turning to look at the man beside me as if she hadn't even noticed he was there.

"Who are you?" she demands, her hand taking hold of mine.

"I'm Seth. I'm the one who called you," he tells her, and she visibly relaxes before her eyes spark. They move from him, to me, and then back to him, her face going from surprise to... something that looks like approval?

"So you're Twy's sex teacher?" she prompts, her eyes taking in his entire squatted figure. I groan in embarrassment.

"I am," he confirms. "And I'm also one of the owners of the security company next door, which is where your sister fainted."

She turns to look down at me, and the weight of her stare feels too heavy with me lying flat on my back. I start to sit up, and Seth's arm immediately wraps around my back, helping me into a seated position.

"Why were you at a security office?" Astrid asks sharply, but I can already see the spark of fear in her eyes.

I know there's no way to protect her from this now. It wouldn't be safe for her not to know she's in danger. I have no choice but to tell her everything. Taking a deep breath, I do just that. And when I'm finished, I wrap my arms around my older sister's trembling body as she tries her best to keep her tears at bay.

"He found us," she sobs. "He found us, and it's all my fault. I couldn't just listen when you told me I shouldn't worry about working. No, I couldn't just hold off until we knew we were perfectly safe. And now he knows where we live! He's leaving shit on your car!" Her panic grows until her voice is borderline hysterical.

"It's okay, Astrid. Seth and Doc—"

"Why would he leave that on your windshield, Twy? Why let us know he's here and give us a warning?" Her eyes search mine for answers I don't have, and when all I can do is shrug and shake my head, she loses what little control over her emotions she had left.

All this time, even as bruised and beaten down as she was when I first picked her up that night in California, she had never lost control of herself. She'd stayed strong this entire time. Never once had she broken down, not during our long phone conversations when I'd planned to get her out of there, and not during the frustrating time when I was looking for a job. She might've shed a couple tears here and there, but it wasn't the distraught despair we were witnessing now. Brandon finding us must be the straw that finally broke her. To see my big sister this way, I feel absolutely helpless, and without even meaning to, my eyes turn to Seth for support.

But it's Doc who steps in.

I watch wide-eyed as his massive frame folds onto the couch cushion to my left, and in one swift move, he has Astrid in his lap, cradled in his arms. She looks childlike, so small, and curled up as she is with his big body wrapped around her, his voice a tone that would tame the wildest of beasts.

"You are unbreakable. You are much stronger than you believe. And with us between you and him, you are untouchable." He has that air about him as he did before, like what he says is fact. There are no ifs, ands, or buts. If he says she's safe, then the world itself will heed his statement as truth. And sooner than I thought possible, after such an explosion of anguish, her crying softens until there's nothing left but the tears on her face, which Doc wipes away with his thumb. His hand looks so big next to her feminine features, yet his touch is so tender, using a gentleness my sister probably hasn't felt in almost a decade.

Suddenly feeling like I'm peeking in on a private moment,

my cheeks heat and I turn to face Seth. His expression is one of complete shock as his eyes fix on the two people beside me. I clear my throat gently to pull his attention toward me, trying not to disturb Doc and Astrid. I've never seen my sister so peaceful, especially since she's in the arms of a stranger, and I want her to have it for as long as she can.

Seth looks at me, and his face sobers. "For now, we have to make a plan. You ladies need to lie low until we can get everything sorted and figure out a way to take care of Astrid's ex and make sure he'll never bother you again. Why doesn't she come with us on our trip? Get you two out of the city where you can relax," he offers, but my sister speaks up before I can even think about answering.

"No. No way. Last night, I had to hear her going on and on about how excited she was about going away with you, and... what might happen on your trip. I am not getting in the way of that." She shakes her head, sitting up but not moving from Doc's lap.

"You wouldn't be—"

"No!" she interrupts me. "I refuse to be a third wheel. And on top of that, I've already been enough of a burden. Twy, you deserve this getaway after all you've done for me. I'm not going with you." Her voice is full of finality.

"She can stay with me," Doc says to me, and my eyes widen as his move to Astrid, who spins sharply to look at him. "You shouldn't stay at your apartment alone if he knows where you live. You can stay with me. I have a guest bedroom you can use, state of the art security system built by a technological genius—"

"That's me!" Seth stage-whispers behind the back of his hand.

"—and my dog can keep you company while I'm at the office for appointments," Doc finishes.

"Appointments?" Astrid prompts.

"I'm a therapist."

She cocks her head to the side, her eyebrow lifting. "What kind of dog?"

"He's an Australian shepherd," he replies.

Astrid's mouth twists as if she's biting the inside of her cheek, before she finally replies, "Deal." She turns to me. "I'm staying with the giant. You're free to go on your trip."

With everyone staring at me with expectant looks, I feel like I have no choice but to give in. I don't know Doc, but if Seth trusts him, and with my sister agreeing, then I don't really have a say. "If you're sure," I tell Astrid.

"Positive." She nods.

"And we should move our trip up," Seth inserts. "We can tell Roxanne what's going on, and we'll leave immediately."

"That woman is going to hate me. She just hired me, taking this big leap of faith, and now I'm asking for all this time off? I suck so hard." My lips pooch out, disappointed in myself.

"That's what she said," Astrid quips, and I turn to glare at her while the guys laugh.

Seth reaches out and squeezes my hand. "Trust me, doll. Roxanne will understand. She really likes you, and when we tell her your safety is at risk, she'll want us to do everything we can to take care of the problem."

"If you say so," I grumble.

"Okay, so first thing's first. We'll take you ladies back to your apartment so you can get packed, and while you're doing that..." Seth stands and walks over to his desk, where he closes his laptop and slides it into a black backpack before slipping it onto his shoulder. He then reaches beneath his desk and pulls out a small duffel that seems to already be full. "I'll start my research on this bag of dick tips."

Astrid bursts out laughing, and I side-eye her. "Fucking love that movie," she murmurs. When she sees my face show confusion, she rolls her eyes and shakes her head. "I swear, sis. Come on. *Deadpool?*" At my blank expression, she glances up at Seth as he comes to pull me up off the couch. "Please, for the love of all things Marvel, make her watch that while you are gone."

"Consider it done," he replies, wrapping his arm around my waist as we all make our way out of his office. "We can watch it while you're recovering from what I plan on doing to you," he whispers into my ear, quiet enough for only me to hear.

My face heats, but for the first time, it's not out of embarrassment. It's pure desire I feel as I become hyperaware of the way his body is pressed against mine while he helps me down the stairs into the main part of the club. When we exit the building, Doc locks the unmarked door behind us before turning to unlock the black SUV parked along the curb. He then holds open the passenger door for Astrid as she slips into the front seat.

Seth takes my hand, and as we start down the sidewalk, he calls over his shoulder, "Meet you there," and Doc waves as he hops in the driver seat, then drives off in the direction of our apartment building.

When we turn the corner, Seth opens a metal door that leads down a flight of stairs and into a parking garage. Directly at the bottom of the steps is a shiny army-green motorcycle, and my eyes widen when I see him reach for the black helmet hanging off the handlebar. Oh shit. I've never been on one before, and with my nerves already pretty shot from everything that's happened today, I don't know if it's the best time for such an adrenaline rush.

But before I can voice my concern, he pauses midreach, and I see his brow furrow when he glances from the bike then up to my nervous face.

"What?" I squeak, not understanding his hesitation. I may be petrified of the thought of getting on the motorcycle, but now my worry comes from his confused look.

"I didn't even think about it until now. All I was thinking was keeping you with me," he says, but I still don't get where his expression is coming from.

"Um... so I'm already freaked the hell out that you want me to get on that thing, but now you're really starting to scare me. What's wrong?"

"It's a single seat." He gestures toward the padded black leather seat. "I've never ridden with anyone on the back before. Never wanted to either. So I didn't get the extension, extra set of footrests, and the sissy bar."

"The sissy what?" I ask, even as warmth spreads throughout my body that I'm the first person he's ever wanted on his motorcycle with him.

"Sissy bar. It's like the back of a chair to keep you from going off the back," he explains.

"So...?" I drawl.

"So I guess we'll walk to your apartment. We'll take your car to the beach house," he says, his face disappointed.

"You don't have a car?" I ask, surprised.

"Nah. I rarely leave this building. Only places I go are to the grocery store and to your work to restock the club's toys. I have the saddle bags for that, so I really had no use for a car."

"Okay, no big deal." I shrug, not understanding why he looks so upset.

He takes hold of my hand and leads me back up the staircase. "I'll put that on my list of shit to do," he murmurs.

I look up at him as we exit the building once again and start walking toward my apartment complex. "Add what? Buy a car?"

"Fuck no." He chuckles, and my lips twitch as my brow wrinkles in confusion. "Add your second seat."

And even though my heart pounds at the thought of riding on the back of his motorcycle, I can't help the smile that spreads across my face over the fact he called it *my* seat.

Nine

Seth

ONCE WE GET BACK TO TWYLA'S apartment, the air feels frenzied. There's a sense of urgency while the sisters pack, but I can't tell whether it's because they're excited for their separate getaways—I learned Astrid hadn't left their apartment in over two months—or because of their fear over her ex's proximity.

I sit at their mismatched dining table and call Roxanne, letting her know what's going on. Apparently Twyla had told her about Brandon while she was interviewing for her job, so it came as no surprise. I'm kind of pissed Roxanne hadn't told me, but I brush it off, realizing she would've had no reason or right to tell me about one of her employees' personal life.

Doc hands me the keys to his beach house as the girls hug goodbye in the parking garage beneath their complex. I've never been to his place before, but I've seen pictures, and I'm actually looking forward to spending a few days there. I can't even remember the last time I went on vacation. With my parents when I was a teenager, maybe? But what I'm mostly excited about is spending time with Twyla, having her all to myself without the pressure of her having to learn things for her job.

I know I wanted to wait a while, to cherish each and every one of our milestones, but we're only human. We'll be spending time together in a romantic setting, alone on a private beach in a bomb-ass house? Yeah, I don't see myself being able to hold out on making her mine. And from what Astrid said in my office, it sounds like Twyla was even telling her sister she was ready. We've known each other for such a short amount of time, though I can't help but feel like fate has something to do with bringing us together.

We wave Doc and Astrid off as they pull out of the parking spot next to Twyla's car, where we toss our bags in her trunk, and I give her a small smile as she turns to face me when I see her nervous look. She must be feeling the same things I am, being left alone after such a whirlwind of a morning—anxiousness over what will happen, excitement over getting to know each other intimately.

She pulls keys out of her purse and holds them in her palm. "Before I hand you these... I know guys all think they are the best drivers and can do no wrong, but honestly, are you a safe driver? I get anxious with other people driving me, like full on panic attacks. As long as you promise not to drive like one of those douche nozzles who weave in and out of traffic, and don't ride people's asses, and don't mess with your phone while you're in the driver seat, then I will trust you and let you drive.

Otherwise, tell me now, and I'll be the one to take us, with you as the navigator."

I hold my right hand up, glance around to make sure no one is nearby, and then give her a wicked grin as I place my left on one of her breasts, watching her eyes widen and her face flush. "I swear on this perfect titty that I will get us safely to the beach house. I will follow your rules of non-douche-nozzleness, and I'll even let you hold my phone so you can use my GPS to be my super sexy navigator."

She laughs, batting my hand away as she gives me the keys. "They're not gone even a full minute, and we've already hit second base," she murmurs, and I burst out laughing as she circles the car to get into the passenger seat.

"Not yet, doll," I tell her, and her brow furrows. "Boob grabs are still first base."

She shakes her head. "No way. First base is kissing. Second base is... fondling. Third is... private area stuff. And then going all the way is a home run."

I back out of the parking spot and then exit the underground garage, pulling out on the street that will take us all the way to the east coast. "Negative, Ghost Rider. First base is kissing and fondling. Second base is touching below the belt. Third base is oral sex. And fucking is a home run." I word it like that just to watch her squirm. She doesn't disappoint.

"Oh," is all she says.

I chuckle, pressing my thumb to the button on my phone to unlock it and then touch the GPS app. I quickly type in the address for Doc's beach house and then hand her my cell. "There you go, navigator. As sworn on your booby."

Twyla

THE NEXT TWO and a half hours go by fast. We take turns showing each other our favorite music, and I feel my insides warm at his approval when he discovers I love rock more than anything. I love the look of surprise on his face when I sing all the lyrics to my favorite Sevendust, Killswitch Engage, and Avenged Sevenfold songs, and the laughter he lets out when I even nail the screamo parts when we listen to Disturbed's "Down with the Sickness."

As the song ends, he lowers the volume on my radio. "You just gained back like 75 percent of the points you lost for not getting any of my movie references. You're officially my dream girl," he tells me, and I grin.

"It's the only music that would help keep me awake while I was trying to study in college, and then when I would work long hours in my lab. I discovered the System of a Down station on my Internet radio app, and it was all over. That's all that's on my playlists now," I explain.

"Yep, I'm having your babies." He nods, giving me a wink.

I burst out laughing, only stopping when his phone vibrates, the next direction popping up on the screen. "Take the next exit, and his house should be on the right up the street."

Soon, we pull onto a narrow road with colorful beach houses lining the way. They get fancier and bigger the farther we travel until finally his phone buzzes, flashing that we've arrived at our destination. When I look up at the monstrosity we pull up in front of, my mouth hangs open as I take in the beauty of the huge, white, circular home perched atop massive cylindrical stilts, and as I open up my door, I hear the ocean loud and clear directly behind it.

"Holy fuck," Seth says, coming around the hood of the car to stand and gape at the structure in front of us. "Doc is freaking Iron Man!"

I turn my head to look up at him questioningly.

He gestures at the beach house. "It's... it's fucking Tony Stark's house. Iron Man. Come on. Red and gold armor, glowy light in the middle of his chest that keeps shrapnel from making it into his heart and also powers the suit? Shoots shit out of his palms and flies around?"

I put on a fake look of recognition. "Ohhh! That Iron Man!" When he looks at me surprised, I lift a brow and purse my lips. "No clue who you're talking about."

Suddenly, his arm is around the back of my neck as he yanks me to him, making me squeak as he presses his forehead to mine. "You better be glad you're so fucking cute, or I'd turn your ass as red as Iron Man's armor for that," he growls, his eyes flashing with naughtiness.

I don't know if it's that look or the image he just put into my head, but I melt against him as my panties grow damp. "Well, I guess we'll just have to have another movie marathon so I'll know exactly which shade my butt's going to match," I whisper, stunned at the words that came out of me so easily.

His eyebrows rise, making his gorgeous hazel irises sparkle in the bright sunlight. "No take-backsies. I have a digital copy if Doc doesn't have a hard copy here. It's so happening. *Iron Man*, and then *Deadpool* upon your sister's request. Fuck it. We'll just do a whole Marvel marathon. *Iron Man, Thor, Captain America, The Incredible Hulk, The Avengers*. You've asked for it, woman.

Now you're gonna get it," he taunts, spinning my body to slap me on the ass once before he goes to grab our bags out of the trunk.

My hand shoots to rub my right butt cheek, where the sting is still reverberating straight to my pussy, my mouth hanging open as I gawk at him.

He looks up at me as he closes the trunk and grins his wicked smile. "Now that's the spirit. The perfect width for my—"

"Seth!" I hiss, and then start giggling as two joggers make their way between us on the sidewalk.

As he walks up to me, he takes my hand, bringing it to his lips to kiss my knuckles before leading me up the walkway. "And when we're done watching *Avengers 2,* we'll have a serious discussion on what it would be like for Black Widow to bang Dr. Banner in his Hulk form. I think she'd take it like a champ, but Corbin thinks even Natasha would wimp out," he states sincerely.

I just shake my head. "The Hulk... that's the green guy, right?"

He abruptly stops and puts his hands to his chest, putting on a southern belle voice. "Well, I do declare! Twyla actually knows one of the most recognizable comic book characters ever created! The great Stan Lee could die happy in this moment."

I roll my eyes and smack him on his rock-hard pec, making him laugh as he starts walking again, and I follow him up the front steps to the spacious porch that seems to wrap around the perimeter of the house. He unlocks the front door, and as we step inside, we both breathe out a "Whoa!"

If one were to imagine a state of the art, magazine-worthy beach house interior, it wouldn't even compare to what we're looking at right now. As we take a tour of the four-bedroom three-bathroom home, I'm already trying to think up a reason why Doc should let Astrid and me move in. And when we step inside the theater room, with its four rows of leather couches, popcorn machine, fully stocked mini fridge, and an entire wall of every movie ever made, I'm pretty sure Seth is too.

"I think... I just came... in my pants," he says, and my eyes unconsciously move to the zipper of his jeans. "Made ya look, dirty girl. Now, let's get our bathing suits on. I haven't been swimming in half a decade."

Ten

Seth

ASIDE FROM THE WAY TODAY BEGAN, it's been one of the greatest days I can remember. Definitely the best day of my adult life. What could be better than spending a few hours lying out in the sand with the most beautiful woman I've ever met, half naked in her dark blue high-waisted bikini, playing out in the waves like children, before coming inside for an early dinner?

That's easy. Pulling a sandy Twyla into the double-headed shower with me, where we stand under the spray making out like a couple of teenagers. I don't try to get her out of her bikini; I just enjoy the heat that enters her eyes as she watches me soap up and rinse off before leaving her to finish up showering alone. When I see the look of disappointment cross her perfect features as I wrap the towel around my waist to head to the bedroom to grab my workout shorts out of my duffle bag, I know tonight will be the night I will make her mine.

A little while later, a wet-haired Twyla finds me in the theater with a bucket of freshly popped buttery popcorn and two bottles of water. She'll need to hydrate for what I have planned later. She's dressed in a tank and jean shorts, her glasses perched on the now sun-kissed bridge of her nose. She sits down on the leather couch next to me and draws her legs and bare feet up beneath her. As she snuggles into my side, it makes me realize home doesn't necessarily have to be a place, but a person, and it's becoming clear she's that for me.

I push Play, and she reaches into the popcorn, pulling out a handful right as I push the button to dim the lights when the opening scene of *Iron Man* comes on, her giggle making me grin like a fool. And as she falls asleep not even halfway through, I just take it all in. The feel of her warm body lying against me. The clean scent of her drifting up into my nose until I just want to bury my face into her skin and inhale her enough that the smell stays there forever. That same fierce protectiveness that hasn't waned since I first met her. And if I could be granted a wish, I'd want to experience this every day for the rest of my life.

When the movie ends, I move carefully from beneath Twyla, gently stretching her out along the couch for her to finish her nap. With the craziness this morning, and then our long drive and hours out in the sun, she deserves the rest. So I go into Doc's office, plopping down into the computer chair to get some work done.

"What is it, doll?" I ask, feeling her presence before I actually see her an hour later. When I glance up from the computer screen, she's standing at the entrance of the office, leaning against the doorjamb, her eyes drinking in my shirtless torso.

Her gaze lifts to mine, her face flushed. "You're..." She swallows. "You're seriously freaking hot, Seth. I don't really know if guys like being told they're beautiful, but you really are."

I lean back in my computer chair and pull off my glasses, setting them on the keyboard. I rotate the seat around, my legs widespread, giving her a better view to look her fill. "Thank you," I say, and I mean it. I work hard to keep in shape. I may let myself live a little by having pizza and junk food every once in a while, but most of the time, I'm pretty damn disciplined.

"I uh... I mean, before today, I had never seen you shirtless. I felt you when I'd hug you... through your clothes. And I imagined you would be fit and stuff. But... damn," she breathes, the cleavage above her light-blue tank top turning a pretty shade of pink with her arousal.

I stand, sauntering slowly across the room until I'm looking down on her from my height. "You're the first woman to see me without my shirt in a very long time," I confess, and her brow furrows.

"Really?"

"Yeah. I haven't been with anyone outside the club since I opened it, and I'm never without my uniform when I'm there." I take her hand from where she's got her arms crossed over her breasts, and I place her palm on one of my pecs, watching her eyes heat and her lips turn up in a small smile as I slide it across to the other. I drop my hand from hers, allowing her to do what she wants.

She trails her fingers to the center of my chest, then down, following the light pattern of hair I have on my torso. "What uniform?" she asks, grazing her fingers back up once she reaches my belly button, her eyes following her movement.

"Black pants, black Henley, black hooded mask," I answer, my cock growing painfully hard at her innocent exploration. "No one's ever seen *this* body."

"What do you mean?" she questions, her eyes meeting mine as she continues to pet me. And petting is exactly what she's doing. Her touch is so gentle, so loving as she strokes my chest.

"I only started working out a couple of years ago. Before then, I was way too busy with school to worry about the shape I was in. The food I ate was quick stuff, like Hot Pockets and microwave pizzas, shit that was easy to eat at a computer desk, which I sat at nearly eighteen hours a day. Then I opened the club, and I was fine with the way I was for a while, but then I got really tired of being tired all the time. My stamina..." I trace the line of her jaw and watch her intake of breath. "...was shit. So I got off my ass and did something about it. But since I'm always in my uniform, you're the only woman to see this body," I finish.

"I like this body," she whispers, her hand moving across my collarbone before gliding over my shoulder and then down my bicep. The feel of her skin against mine makes goose bumps rise on my flesh, the sensation as foreign to me as it is to her. "I, um... I don't really know much about fitness."

We've worked ourselves into a sexual trance. The gentleness of her touch is something so far from what I'm used to that it's incredibly erotic. And I can see in the glossiness of her eyes and the short, quick rise and fall of her chest that she's probably just as wet as I am hard.

"Then allow me to teach you, doll," I say, not waiting for her to reply as I dip down and pick her up, making her gasp at the sudden movement. I carry her over to the computer desk, setting her down in the chair. "First, there was lots and lots of research."

I grasp hold of her tank top and swiftly lift it over her head, leaving her in her plain nude bra and jean shorts. I see the smallest bit of fear in her eyes, but I continue because it's overpowered by the look of excitement on her flawless face. I spread her legs and get down on my knees between them, fitting my body there until we're face-to-face. "I had to learn about all the parts of my body, the different muscle groups, all the exercises to do for each one, which ones I could work together."

I run my left hand down her right arm until I reach her fingers, then place her palm on my shoulder, leaning back until her arm is straight. I trail across her skin with my fingertips and then my lips as I name, "Forearms... biceps... triceps..."

She shivers, and I smile against her skin, seeing the light hairs on her arms stand up. "Shoulders..." I nip her there, skimming my teeth to the place where her shoulder meets her neck. "Traps..." I spend some time here when she whimpers then gasps, clearly loving the feel of my beard against her sensitive flesh, before moving on.

I reach around her body and unhook her bra with ease. She drops her hand from my shoulder in order to let the cups fall to the floor next to the computer chair. "Pectorals," I whisper, and lower my face to her breasts, and my own breath stutters as the softest skin I've ever felt grazes my cheeks. When I take one nipple into my mouth, her body folds around me as she cries out, holding me to her.

If she were a sub and I was her Dom, I would've never allowed this. She would hold perfectly still and let me take what I wanted from her, while she accepted only what I wanted to give her. But in this moment, with her cradling my head while I suckle at her deliciously generous breast, her breath coming in sharp gasps,

I let her grasp onto me. Because not only does it feel like she's holding on for dear life, it feels like she's the only thing keeping me from floating away on a fucking high. Her scent and taste are like a drug, and she's got me completely intoxicated.

I let go of her nipple with a pop, and she loosens her hold. I trail my tongue downward, over her stomach, until I reach her belly button, where I dip it inside before whispering there, "Abdominals."

As I reach for the button of her denim shorts, her hands come to rest on my shoulders, and I look up her body and into her eyes to see if she's going to push me away. I have just enough self-control left that if she were to ask me right this second, I would be able to force myself to stop. But after I get her out of her clothes, I can't make any promises. She bites her lip as she stares down at me, and as she tightens her grip on my shoulders, she nods.

I unbutton, unzip, and then slide her shorts down her smooth legs until all she's left in are her mint-green panties. I meet her eyes once again, a small smile tugging at my lips. "You wore green?"

"Yeah. I know it's your favorite color, and...."

"And?" I prompt, my hands drifting up the backs of her calves, making her eyelids go half-mast.

"And because green means go," she whispers, her hands dropping to the armrests and her head falling back against the chair as I grip the backs of her knees to pull her ass closer to the edge of the seat.

I chuckle, "That it does, doll," and move away just far enough that when I lift her leg up, her ankle rests on my shoulder. "And that brings us to legs." I kiss up her perfectly smooth, lightly tan calf then lick down the inside of her thigh, stopping midway to nibble the soft flesh there.

She whimpers again, her hips rotating against the seat. The helpless sound sets off something carnal inside me, and in one swift move, I dip my shoulder, her foot falling to the floor as I grip her hips and flip her over. Before she can even take her next breath, the upper half of her body is facedown on the computer chair, and her knees are on the carpet, her ass against the front of my workout shorts.

I groan, unable to stop myself from grinding against the globes covered only by the thin green fabric of her panties. And it's not until I feel her press back against me that I snap out of my trance, unused to a woman moving without my explicit permission. My sweet, innocent, shy little doll lets her instincts take over as she arches her back, trying to get as close to my cock as she can with the flimsy clothing between us. But instead of earning a punishment for taking such liberty, I reward her for giving in to her body's desire by continuing the lesson.

I lean over her, whispering, "Back," as I rub my bearded cheek down her spine, feeling her soft skin erupt in chills as I back up on my knees until my face reaches her ass. I sit up, gripping the elastic of her panties, and watch all her muscles tense. "And finally..." I pull the light-green fabric down until they reach her knees, leaving them there as my hands glide back up her thighs and over her round cheeks, and hiss, "...glutes."

I grip her there, my fingers gently digging into her flesh, massaging the muscles beneath her buttery soft skin. I can't get enough of touching her. The feel of my hands on her, the things it's doing not only to my body but to my heart... simply unexplainable. It makes me glad I never shared this with anyone else. It's like I was unconsciously saving this part of myself to give to *the one*, the same way Twyla is giving her virginity to me. A much more meaningful trade than the exchange of power I'm used to.

When she's completely melted into the seat, her muscles lax, her arms hanging limply over the sides of the chair, I know she's wholly given in. She's mine for the taking, yet I can't help but feel I'm giving myself to her as well.

I stand and then lift her into my arms, looking into her beautiful, totally relaxed face. She meets my eyes almost sleepily, and I smile, knowing I was the one to make her look so blissful without the use of anything but my hands.

"Where we going?" Her voice is quiet, like she's trying not to disturb the state we're both in.

I carry her out of the room, down the hallway, and into the kitchen, which is dark except for the light above the stove. It's bright enough I can see her perfectly, but not so much that it would make her self-conscious for what I have planned. "Well, after all my research about the different muscle groups and the exercises I'd need to do, I then learned about the food I needed to start eating in order to fuel my body." I set her on the kitchen island, grinning at her sharp gasp as her ass hits the cold marble. "Which then led to meal prep," I tell her, my voice turning wicked as I force her all the way back until she's lying across the countertop, looking like my very own buffet of perfect, creamy flesh.

"I buy all the groceries..." I pull the barstool out. "Cook all my healthy, protein-rich food..." I take a seat where she's got her knees clamped shut, her body trembling. "Put it into individual meal size containers to last me the week...."

I take her dangling feet and place them on top of my thighs before moving my hands to just above her knees, whispering for her to relax as she allows me to open her up to me. Like the rest of her, she's beautiful here too. And when I lean down to press a kiss to the inside of her thigh, the scent of her clean skin mixed with her fresh arousal hits me, making me groan. I grasp the backs of her knees and yank, a feminine squeak leaving her as I bring her ass to the edge of the counter, her glistening bare pussy mere inches from my face.

She pants, her breasts rising and falling with the quick work of her lungs. I know I should probably do or say something to soothe her, but her innocence, her genuine nervousness of the unknown, is invigorating. She trusts me to make this good for her, and my heart pounds with excitement as I plan to do just that.

"And every day, five times a day, I devour my meal."

With that, I wrap my arms beneath her legs, feeling the softness of her thighs land on my shoulders, and lean in to take the first languid swipe of my tongue up from the very bottom of her entrance, not stopping until I circle her clit. Her whole body jerks as if she's been electrocuted, sucking in air as her hands shoot to my wrists, squeezing with all the strength in her little body. I glance up her luscious form to find her head lifted, her eyes meeting mine just as I suck her into my mouth. Her eyes go wide and her brow furrows as her lips part.

It's been over five years since I went down on a woman. Besides never having the desire to do so—the act is far more intimate and personal than anything I do at the club—my mask wouldn't allow me to anyway. The expression on her face mixed with knowing she can see me and what I'm doing is erotic as fuck, and that animalistic feeling consumes me once again. I set upon her soaking wet heat like a starved man, licking, sucking, dragging my teeth over her sensitive nub, loving the sexy moans and little sighs coming from her as she now presses her head back against the countertop.

I pull back a moment and watch her throb, seeing my aggression and beard against her delicate flesh have turned her red. "Such a pretty pussy," I whisper, and she shudders.

Her whimper of disappointment that I've stopped my assault pulls me back in, and as we both discover that her favorite thing is the small, rhythmic circles I draw with the tip of my tongue around her clit, I use my thumbs to pull back her hood, exposing her even more to me. Soon, she goes completely silent, and I can tell she's holding her breath, because every so often she exhales sharply then gulps more air. Her eyes are closed, her face a mask of total concentration, and as her nails dig into my forearms and her back arches, I know I've got her. I flatten my tongue against her swollen bud, giving her three long strokes before sucking her clit between my lips, and her entire body convulses as she comes. I cover her pussy with my mouth, creating a suction as she cries out toward the ceiling, the taste of her juices making me groan in pleasure. My hands grip her thighs as she grinds against my face, and I nearly come in my shorts as she lets go of all her inhibitions.

I lap at her pussy lips, making sure I get every last drop of her, before letting her legs fall off my shoulders as I stand. I grasp hold of her wrists and pull her up to sitting, and then pick her up, her legs automatically locking around my hips and her arms around my neck. Her body is on fire as her naked front plasters to mine, all her soft parts molding to the hard planes and bulges of my torso.

She clings to me, her face burying in the side of my neck as I start to move, carrying her past the living room, down the hallway, and into the home gym. An overwhelming sense of protectiveness comes over me, along with a possessiveness I've never felt in all my life. I feel like I would do anything for the woman cradled in my arms, who holds on to me like I'm her greatest possession.

As I make my way to the back of the room, I flip on the switches to the bathroom, which casts light right where I plan on taking her—the thickly padded mats in front of the wall of mirrors.

I grip her ass as I get down on my knees on the mat before laying us down, my weight pressing her back against the blue vinyl. I look down at her, and she meets my eyes with a languid smile.

"Research, meal prep, and now...?" she murmurs, her fingers toying with the back of my short hair.

I lean down, trailing my nose up the column of her throat, and then kiss her right below her ear, smirking when I feel her shiver. "And now... we put our muscles to work," I whisper, before sitting up on my knees. Putting my thumbs in my shorts' waistband, I slide them down over my hips and pull them all the way off, my eyes never leaving her face. I memorize her expression. It's the first time she's ever seen a man naked, in the flesh, and the first time a woman has ever seen me completely unclothed, my cock bare. Her eyes go half-mast as she bites her lip, taking in every inch of me. I let her look her fill, while I glide my hands up and down the outside of her thighs, her knees pointing toward the ceiling.

When she starts to squirm, I reach for my shorts, grabbing

the condom I had put in the pocket earlier, knowing I'd be waiting for the perfect moment to finally make her mine. But her whispered, "Seth," pulls my eyes from the black package to her worried face.

"What is it, doll?" I ask gently, praying to any god listening that she doesn't tell me she isn't ready for this.

"I um..." She reaches her hand up to brush her dark hair away from her face. She blows out an anxious breath before finally reaching for my hand, and when I lace my fingers with hers, she tugs, and I allow her to pull me back on top of her.

"What is it?" I repeat, murmuring it against the sensitive skin of her neck, her nipples pebbling against my chest as my hair tickles the rose-colored peaks.

"I... I'm on the pill. My doctor put me... um... anyway.... I..." She blows out a breath, clearly frustrated with her nervous stuttering. I sit up to look down into her beautiful face, my own showing nothing but patience as I wait for her to speak. Seeing that, she finally gathers her courage. "I'm giving you my virginity, and in return, I want you to give me something as well," she says quietly.

"And what's that?" I ask gently, my face going soft.

"You said you've never been with a woman without wearing one"—she takes the condom from my hand and holds it between us—"before. And since I've never been with anyone, it would sort of... feel like it's your first time too."

"Are you sure, doll? It will be special for me even if I wear it, because it's with you. I've never made love to anyone, and that's exactly what I'm doing with you, beautiful Twyla," I tell her, kissing her gently before letting her reply.

"I'm sure. I want to feel only you inside me," she whispers, and her words make that protective and possessive feeling multiply a hundredfold.

I rest my forehead against hers and nod, and she sets the condom on the floor before wrapping her arm around my neck. I kiss her deeply, reaching between us to find her dripping core. She sucks in a breath through her nose as I press one finger inside her, curving it upward before dragging it out again. After several strokes, I add another finger, feeling her arm tighten around me before eventually relaxing once more as I ready her.

Using her wetness, I coat the head of my cock and line it up with her entrance, continuing to kiss her like my life depends on it, hoping it'll distract her at least a little bit from the pain I'm about to cause. Slowly, I begin to sink into her, and I feel her hand that's still holding mine tighten. I squeeze her fingers, my tongue dueling with hers as her breath hisses in and out, faster the deeper I push.

"So fucking tight," I murmur against her lips as she whimpers. "So hot and wet. I've never felt anything like you. So fucking perfect, doll."

When I'm planted all the way to the hilt, I hold perfectly still, allowing her to adjust to my size, at the same time trying to keep control of myself at the new sensations. I close my eyes and take it all in, everything before seeming muted, like a black-and-white film that's now been technicolored and remastered. Soon enough, her fingers loosen between mine and the arm around my neck relaxes, and feeling her press a soft kiss to my lips, I open my eyes to meet hers.

"You okay?" I whisper, and her eyes go soft as she nods gently. I let go of her hand, bracing my elbows on either side of her head. "Wrap your arms around my lower back. You control how fast I go," I instruct, pulling out of her slightly, and when I feel her hands press there, I know she understands and is ready for me to move.

With the subtle guidance of her palms pushing and her fingertips digging, I let her lead me in our erotic dance, enjoying the slow pace she sets as I feel every inch of her blazing heat as it surrounds my cock. Before long, her fingers trail up my spine, sending a shiver throughout my body as she grips onto my biceps caging in her head. She turns her face to press it into my muscle there, muffling her cries of pleasure as I pick up speed, still making sure to keep my movements controlled, even though all I want to do is thrust into her ferociously and mark her in some way.

"Please," she begs, her legs wrapping around my hips.

"What do you want, baby?" I whisper into her ear, pressing a kiss below her lobe.

"I..." She lifts her hips. "I need...."

"What do you need, Twyla?" My beard tickles the soft flesh of her neck, making her moan. I know what she needs, a little something extra to help send her over the edge, but I won't give it to her until she asks for it.

"I don't know, Seth," she whimpers, and hearing her say my name—my real name—while I'm inside her makes me shudder with ecstasy, sending me into a powerful thrust that makes her wince then groan. "That. More of that. Please."

"Kiss me," I demand, and she turns her face upward as my lips land on hers. The kiss turns savage as I slide my right hand down her body until I grip her hip, lifting her to meet my unrestrained plunges into her soaked, viselike pussy.

"Oh God!" she cries, breaking our mouths apart as her nails

sink into my biceps. Her eyes flash, almost panicked at the intensity of our lovemaking, until her body bows beneath mine, her chin pointing to the ceiling as her inner muscles clamp around my cock while she comes.

It's like nothing I've ever felt before, and I let out a feral growl when my teeth land at the side of her throat as I empty myself into her. I have just enough self-control not to clamp down on her delicate flesh, sucking on her instead as I rock against her until our aftershocks have subsided, the sound of our ragged breaths filling the home gym. I pull my face away, making sure I wasn't too rough, breathing a sigh of relief when I see nothing but a slight hickey on her neck.

As I let her hips lower to the mat beneath us, I brush her hair away from her face as I look down into her beautiful but tearful blue eyes. My heart thuds with remorse. "Twyla, baby, did I hurt you?" I take hold of her chin to move her head to the side to take a closer look at the mark, but even in the better light I see it's nothing more than a little bruise that'll be gone within the hour. I face her back toward me, stroking her cheek as a tear escapes her left eye, making my gut clench. "Talk to me, doll," I whisper.

"Nothing is wrong," she tells me, wrapping her arms around my neck, and her soft smile is the only thing that makes me believe she's not trying to hide anything by calling it nothing. "I... I feel silly. But I was just so full of emotions that it spilled out of my eyes, I guess. I'm sorry I'm such a girl. I didn't know it would be like this." She lets out a single, quick burst of laughter that makes another tear fall, and I feel my entire body relax. I know exactly what she means. It happened quite often with the subs at Club Alias.

But I refuse to think of anyone else while I'm still buried

inside my woman. And that's exactly what she is—my woman. I decide now is as good a time as any to update her on this new information.

"No need to apologize, doll. I feel the same way." I nuzzle her neck, making her shiver when my beard scratches over the hickey there. "You're mine now, Twyla," I whisper against her ear. "There's no way I could let you go after this."

I feel her pussy spasm around me, and I lift my head to look at her. Her eyes sparkle up at me, as she bites her lip. And then she grins when she murmurs, "Ditto."

I drop my jaw, my face showing nothing but surprise. "Did you just respond with a movie quote, or was that just a coincidence again?"

She rolls her eyes, and I feel her playing with my hair at the back of my head. "I've seen *Ghost*, silly," she scoffs.

"My God, I'm so hot for you right now," I tease, thrusting forward gently and watching her eyes flare. And then it's like something dawns on her suddenly, and she reaches her hand up to run her fingers gently over her neck.

"You bit me," she accuses, but her face shows no anger.

"I did," I confirm with a nod.

"Why'd you bite me?" she questions, a small smile tilting up the corners of her lips.

"I promised to be open and honest with you, doll, and I didn't want to be a liar. I told you the day I met you I wouldn't bite until lesson three." I give her a wicked grin, and she squeezes her eyes shut and loudly laughs toward the ceiling, making her inner muscles ripple around my returning erection.

"Speaking of lesson three...." I carefully withdraw from her body, trying my best not to cause her any discomfort, proud of myself for instinctively knowing how to be gentle with her when it's far from what I've ever been before. She stretches like a cat as I hurry into the bathroom, grabbing a washcloth and running the water in the sink until it gets hot before carrying it back over to her. I kiss her as I press the cloth to her core, feeling her shiver. I tenderly clean her up before wiping off the mat so she doesn't have to see the mess we made together, reminding myself to use the disinfecting spray and paper towels to clean more thoroughly when I wake up in the morning to work out.

Right now, all I'm worried about is continuing with our lesson.

Eleven

Twyla

Tʜᴇ ɴᴇxᴛ ᴍᴏʀɴɪɴɢ, I ʀᴏʟʟ ᴏᴠᴇʀ in the giant bed and stretch with a groan, feeling every single sore spot on my body but smiling when I remember where they all came from.

After Seth made love to me for the first time in the gym, he carried me into the sauna, spreading me out on the wooden bench before soothing my swollen pussy with his mouth. He claimed after research, meal prep, and working out, muscle recovery should come next, which included sweating out toxins by relaxing in a sauna. And sure enough, the sweat poured off me as he brought me to another orgasm, a feat I never thought possible in such a short amount of time.

Afterward, and the last step in this hands-on lesson, he gathered up my melted body and carried me into the bathroom, where he used his muscular frame to prop me against the cold tiled wall of the shower. The cool surface felt incredible against my feverish skin, and I let him do as he pleased as he lathered me up, taking great care to be super gentle between my legs.

I have never in my life felt more taken care of. He treated me like a queen, worshiping every square inch of my body until not a single pore went without a caress or a kiss. He wrapped me up in a soft terry robe and handed me a towel for my hair, and when it was up on top of my head like a turban, he scooped me up once more to carry me to the guest bedroom. We'd decided when we first arrived after touring the beach house that we would respect Doc's master suite and chose the one across the hall from it, which was just as luxurious.

And this is where I now lie, sprawled naked between the cool sheets, realizing I'm alone. I prop my head up, seeing it's only 7:33 a.m. I force myself to stand, put on my glasses, and slip into the robe laying on the foot of the bed before going in search of Seth.

I find him in the office like I had last night, his shirtless back facing me as he hunches toward the computer screen. As I come up next to him, I reach out and run my hand up and down his spine, smiling when I see his skin erupt in goose bumps as he looks up at me through his reading glasses.

"Good morning, beautiful," he says, and with one swift move, his arm wraps around me and he yanks me into his lap. I suck in a sharp breath and wince as my bottom hits his muscular thighs. "Ooo, sorry. You sore?" He puts his hand between my legs, cupping me gently, the heat of his palm soothing the ache there.

"A little tender. What are you working on?" I ask, pressing a kiss to his bearded cheek.

"Your case."

My muscles tense as I turn toward the computer, but I can't figure out what I'm looking at. "What's going on?"

"Doc and I are trying to figure out where Brandon is while he's in town so we can serve him with a restraining order. Since he lives in California, it would be pointless to have it sent to his home address while he's on the other side of the country," he explains.

"Do you think that would be enough to make him leave us alone? Just a piece of paper telling him to stay away?" I ask, not so sure of the answer myself.

"We've done a background check. He has no prior arrests. No calls to the address for domestic violence. Just a couple of speeding tickets. And since your sister never filed a police report about her assault, we're going to have to get crafty, because of the pesky burden of proof we have to have in order to file for the restraining order." He takes his glasses off and tosses them on the keyboard.

"I took pictures of Astrid when she was all bruised up," I offer.

"That will definitely help." He nods. "And we've got the letter he left on your windshield. I told Doc to ask your sister if she has any e-mails or text messages saved from Brandon that could be used as well."

"And then what?"

"When the restraining order gets approved and we have him served, we hope for the best, that he'll choose to wisely tuck his tail and move on," Seth says, nuzzling his face into my neck.

"But if not?" I question, my heart thudding in my chest.

"You let me worry about that, doll."

"But—"

"To paraphrase the badass Bryan Mills, portrayed by the

great Liam Neeson in *Taken*..." Seth drops his voice and looks me dead in the eye, his face solemn. "What I do have are a very particular set of skills. Skills I have acquired over a very long career. Skills that make me a nightmare for people like him. I will look for him, I will find him, and I will kill him."

My eyes grow wide. "Are... are you serious?" I whisper, unable to tell if he really is just quoting another movie. He seemed so sincere as he said the words. If he's not being serious, he'd give a damn good Oscar-winning performance if he ever went into acting.

His face softens only slightly. "*Me?* No. I only handle the technical side of the business. Although, that side still has the ability to make someone's life a living hell." He winks.

There's something in the way he's looking at me that tells me there's more to what he's saying than just the words he's speaking. And then I remember him saying in his office yesterday morning that there was a story behind his security team he wasn't ready to tell me about yet.

"But one of your partners...?" I prompt.

His face stoic, he turns to his computer. The man has a poker face like none I've ever seen before. I can read not a single emotion cross his face or in his eyes as he silently thinks about how to reply. When he finally does, my stomach drops.

"I think it's time we have a little talk."

I nod, and he swivels the computer chair—the same chair he had me face-down on not twelve hours ago as he undressed me for the first time—and stands, placing me on my feet. He takes my hand and leads me through the beach house. We stop in the kitchen, the weight of the air pressing down on me as the tension builds, wondering just what the hell he's going to tell me.

Seth grabs a bottle of champagne out of the refrigerator, along with a bottle of orange juice that wasn't there last night. He must've gone to the store this morning before I woke up. Pulling two flutes down from a cabinet, he mixes each of us a mimosa before replacing the ingredients back into the fridge. He hands me one of the glasses and holds my other hand as he pulls me out onto the back porch. It's almost like he doesn't want to let go of me for fear I will run. Could what he's about to say really be that bad?

We sit down on the swing, the salty air filling my lungs as I take a sip of my drink. He pulls me close against his side, resting his arm along the back of the seat. Taking a deep breath, he begins.

"Doc had been following my educational career since he saw me in an article when I was sixteen. By then, I was only two years away from getting my masters at MIT. When I graduated, he approached me with an idea. He'd been a therapist for several years, and the work was getting to him. He could help all his clients the way he had been trained to do, but something kept him up at night. There were several victims of sexual assault whose attackers were never held accountable for their actions. More often than not, these terrible people were getting off with minimal punishment, if any. He offered me a job. In the beginning of our partnership, using my computer skills, we made these men pay in our own way. Draining their bank accounts and giving the money to the victims. Public humiliation done by an anonymous source. Things like that." He puts his mimosa to his lips and drains the flute in one gulp, setting the glass down on the wicker table next to the swing.

"But then came Sandra," he says, his voice low. "Sandra and

her college roommate had been assaulted by their boss at their job at a supermarket a few towns away from where we live. Sandra went to the police to file a report alone because her roommate just wanted to forget it ever happened. Turns out nothing ever came about from the rape kit they did on Sandra as she waited too long to have it done. And it probably didn't help her case that her boss was the police chief's brother. Being discouraged, too ashamed of what had happened to pursue anything further, she gave up and decided to go to therapy, which is when she found Doc. The girls quit working there, found new jobs, but her roommate became depressed. Sandra tried to get her to come with her to therapy, but her friend refused, turning to self-medicating instead. She ended up OD'ing while Sandra was away visiting her parents. When she came home, she found her with the needle in her arm."

I gasp, tears filling my eyes for what the two girls had been through. I can't even imagine something like that happening to me and feeling like there was nothing I could do about it, my attacker getting away with it scot-free.

"As you can imagine, Sandra's world went from pretty shitty to begin with, to bottoming out. Not only was she in therapy, trying to heal from being raped, but now her best friend, the girl she lived with, worked with, had been through everything with, had taken her own life," Seth tells me, shaking his head. "She was beyond therapy, and her family feared she too would end her life, so they had her committed.

"Something inside Doc snapped. And when he told me the story, we mutually agreed taking this guy out our normal way just wouldn't be enough." He glances at me, as if to see my reaction. I don't know what he finds written in my expression, but whatever it is, he continues on. "That's when we hired Glover. Doc had been following his career the way he had mine, and Corbin's as well, who was eventually brought on a few years ago."

Seth goes silent, and when I look up at his handsome profile, he's staring out at the ocean, his poker face back in place. I take a breath and finally find the courage to ask, "And what were Glover and Corbin hired to do?" I have a feeling I already know the answer, but I want to hear him explain it.

I see his Adam's apple bob as he swallows, the only hint that he's struggling to tell me the truth.

"We have a code," he replies instead of answering my question directly. "We only take out the people who deserve it, the ones who escape justice unfairly." He pauses, seeming to search his mind for his next words. "Last year, do you happen to remember the case about the swimmer who was charged with drugging, raping, and murdering a girl at his frat party? It made national news."

Something niggles at my memory, and my brow furrows. "I don't watch the news, but I think I recall some of my coworkers talking about it. Something about him getting off with a super light sentence?"

"Yep, that's the one," he confirms.

"Wait... didn't he end up killing himself?" I can't remember specifics. I normally tuned out the people gossiping while I was trying to work.

"Not quite. This motherfucker had drugged, raped, and ended up smothering this poor girl to death, and because he was a rich little prick who had daddy's money to hire the best defense lawyers around, he got off with only a few months in jail. That's when we were hired to take care of things," he tells me, his voice full of conviction. "Long story short, no one really questioned it when they found the former swim team captain floating dead in a pool he'd been practicing in after-hours. The head injury was accurate to one caused by someone miscalculating and running into the pool wall. Everyone just assumed it was karma doing its thing. The way all of our jobs play out."

I absorb everything he tells me, bracing myself for the horror of sitting next to a man who helps kill people for a living to sink in.

And yet it never comes.

In fact, what I feel right now is nowhere near horror. It's closer to... pride? Yes, pride. The wonderful man sitting next to me is part of a team doing something any human with a conscience would fantasize about doing, doling out justice to those who escape persecution.

"You're a vigilante," I breathe, and his eyes meet mine.

"Mercenary, doll. We get paid for it. But I'd still do it in a heartbeat for these victims' families, even if they couldn't afford our services. But they pay without hesitation, because we do for them what they are too scared to do themselves, or in most cases, what they lack the skills to do themselves. We've perfected the art of making it look like an accident. As long as we don't veer off of our strict policy, a life for a life, then we have nothing to worry about," he explains.

"And you've never actually... taken care of one of these people yourself? Like, you only stay behind the scenes?" I clarify.

"Correct. I do all the legwork. Surveillance, digging into backgrounds... anything that can be found and used through technology. I help set up a strategy, and Corbin and Glover do the dirty work." He shrugs. "I promised you open and honest. This is my truth. There's only one other person besides our team who knows who we are and what we do, and that's Corbin's wife. With my skill set, I'm able to keep us completely anonymous and under the radar."

I narrow my eyes. "That's why you never came up in my Internet search. I couldn't believe a child genius who went to MIT when he was twelve wouldn't be in some kind of news article."

He grins as he nods before his face sobers once again. "I know this sounds crazy because we haven't known each other that long, but I feel like fate has something to do with all of this. You literally lived on the other side of the country, and somehow you managed to run away to the very town where I live, and got a job working at one of only two places I go outside my club. I'm a fucking genius and I can't even begin to calculate those odds. Too many coincidences. I know it has to be fate." His arm that's around the back of the swing comes forward, and he takes my hand, bringing it up to his lips as he speaks against my knuckles. "What I've confided in you is my way of telling you I trust you, and I hope you take me seriously when I say I'm never letting you go. I would've never told you any of this if I wasn't sure you are the one I want to be with."

It's this confession that makes me gulp and take a deep breath more than anything else. Not the fact the man I just gave myself to last night has turned out to be a mercenary who assists in killing people for a paycheck. No. It's that this handsome, incredibly sexy, ridiculously smart, caring, hilarious, wonderful man is telling me that he wants... me. Just me. Where I don't find myself particularly special in any sort of way, he makes me feel extraordinary. And it's as I'm swelling with the emotions he's brought out of me with the trust he's put into me, I blurt out the only thing swirling inside my mind that makes any sense.

"I love you, Seth."

I feel the air leave his lungs through his nose across the back of my hand as his eyes shut, still holding my knuckles pressed to his lips. And just as I'm starting to feel unsure about this whole open and honest thing, I squeak as I'm suddenly midair and straddling Seth as I face him on the swing. One of his hands shoots into my hair at the back of my neck as the other presses against my lower back. His strong arms pull until I am plastered to him, not even a breath of air between our fronts as he attacks my mouth with a passion so powerful I feel it down to my very soul.

He breaks our kiss just long enough to reply, "I love you, Twyla," before he nips at my bottom lip, drawing it into his mouth before letting it go to soothe with his tongue.

And then he stands, my legs wrapping around his waist as he carries me back to the beach house and to the bedroom. Where he makes love to me until I can't figure out when one day ends and another begins.

Twelve

Twyla

Three days later

"PERFECT TIMING. AS LONG AS WE don't make any pit stops, I'll be able to run home to change and make my shift at six," I say, glancing down at the GPS.

"I still say you should just go back tomorrow, doll. What's one more day?" Seth grumbles.

With the pictures I'd taken of Astrid with her black eye and bruised ribs, combined with some screenshots of hateful messages from her ex she'd kept after changing her phone number, along with the letter that had been left on my windshield, we'd had enough evidence to be granted the restraining order. Seth had been able to narrow down Brandon's location in about an hour using the security camera footage from my apartment complex's garage that captured the license plate number of the car he was renting, tracking him to a hotel a couple of towns away. He was served this morning.

With the restraining order in place and eyes on Astrid's ex, I wanted to get back to a somewhat normal routine. For the next couple of nights, just to be safe, she would continue to stay at Doc's, since Brandon didn't know the location, just until we were sure he was on his way back to California. And I could finally get back to work. As much as I loved every single uninterrupted second I spent with Seth at the beach, there was an annoying little voice in my head telling me I was letting Roxanne down after she'd been the only one willing to give me a job.

We could all tentatively breathe a little easier knowing my sister was safe. She'd be with someone every minute of the day until he was on the other side of the country, and Imperium Security would have him under surveillance, making sure he did just that. Astrid would finally be able to move on and begin to truly heal. The bruises had faded, but there was no telling what kind of damage he'd left her with mentally. She put on a brave face, but I had a feeling she hid a lot of what she was going through inside her head. She'd been with Brandon for years, suffering emotional abuse for a long time before it had finally erupted into physical. But while her outside healed on its own, it would take a professional to help with the scars inside her.

I change the subject. "So I'm curious," I begin, straight up ignoring his question, since I'd already told him a thousand times I was going back to work tonight and there was nothing he could say to stop me.

He gives me a fake grumpy face before reaching over to squeeze my knee, making me swat at his hand. "Curious about what, lovely Twyla?"

"What made you get into BDSM?" I ask, turning in my seat to face him more.

He frowns for a minute, rubbing the back of his neck with one hand while continuing to steer with the other. "You want the Doc version or the Seth version?"

"How about both?"

He chuckles, relaxing back against his seat. "The Seth version is much simpler. I'm a kinky motherfucker who gets off on control. I'm a sadist. I get pleasure from inflicting certain types of pain on a willing submissive."

My head tilts to the side as I eye him closely. "See, I don't get that. You're so... gentle, so caring with me. I couldn't see you hurting me while we make love."

"Ah, see? You're different. Much, much different, doll. As I said before, I had never made love to anyone before you. My Dom side is nothing like what you've been experiencing the past few days," he tells me, giving me his wicked grin.

The look always makes me clench. "So... are you saying you'd never use your Dom side on me?" I ask, my voice small.

He must sense my disappointment, because he takes my hand and brings it to his lips. "I will let you have whatever side of me you want... except for the backside." He winks, and I burst out laughing, taking my hand back.

"Yeah, no. Don't think I'd be interested in using the butt plug on you that I sold you the night we met." I shake my head. "Okay, so what about the Doc version?" I prompt, getting us back to my original question.

He clears his throat and glances out his window before staring straight through the windshield. "So, preface. Only my partners know my backstory. It's kind of dumb, so don't go feeling sorry for me or anything. Promise?"

br</br>

I reach over and lock his pinky with mine. "Swear. Nothing you could tell me would ever make me feel differently about you, Seth," I tell him, sincerity filling my voice.

He meets my eyes, and my insides melt at the love I see in his. And then he speaks. "I guess that's the truth considering I told you I'm part of a team that kills people for a paycheck and you still let me bone you."

I throw my head back and laugh, swatting his chest and making him grin. "You dick. Okay, so spill," I command, and he cocks an eyebrow sexily.

"Bossy. I thought I was the Dom here. But I've gotta admit, you're fucking hot when you tell me what to do," he teases.

"Seth!" I growl, wanting to know his story.

"All right, all right. So the Doc version is... being a child prodigy"—he pretends to flip hair over his shoulder, making me giggle—"I was always much younger than all the people I went to school with. I was in college when I went through puberty. So when most boys my age were hanging around girls going through the same crazy hormonal changes, I was around women. Sorority chicks. Hot sorority chicks."

I reach over and pinch his nipple, making him yelp. "Watch it," I grumble.

He rubs at his chest, furrowing his brow. "Fuck, woman. You look so sweet and innocent on the outside. I was tricked. Future reference: I am not a masochist. I can dish it, but I can't take it."

"I have no clue what that even means, but continue. Just no more talking about hot sorority chicks. It makes me feel all stabby, and I don't like it," I confess, unfamiliar with this feeling of jealousy.

"So anyway, they basically made a pet out of me. I was young and wanted to be part of the cool crowd, and they used me for my brain. But it was the way they used me that I later realized was so fucked up. I can't tell you how many papers I wrote for other people, let girls cheat off me, gave them brilliant ideas I should have kept for myself to use, all because they'd pretend they liked me. They toyed with me so bad. Showing me their bodies, some even letting me touch. They made me believe they were my friends, a couple acting like they even wanted me, and I'd play right into their hands, doing their work for them. I might've been a genius when it came to book smarts, but I was still just a thirteen-year-old boy."

His voice had turned serious by the end, and I could hear the pain there when he spoke about being used. And suddenly I felt angry and protective over younger Seth, my blood pressure rising at the thought of my sweet and generous man being taken advantage of. How dare those bitches play with his emotions like that, especially with him unaware what they were doing!

He continues, "Doc says when it finally dawned on me what was happening, something inside me switched. By then I was sixteen, and around the same time, I lost my virginity to a twenty-year-old. She asked me to do things to her, spank her, choke her, things I'd seen in porn before but never really thought about doing whenever I would eventually have sex one day. And seeing how I was angry over the way those older students had used me, taking it out on her made me feel pretty damn good. She wanted it, begged for it, even. It was a mutual exchange of power. She got off on the roughness. She let me take back control of myself, and I really fucking liked it."

"So that started when you were sixteen. From the get-go. Wow." I pause, taking in everything he told me. "And then Doc scooped you up a couple years later for his team. Where did Club Alias come from?"

"Well, I told you about how I was nervous about us being able to make enough money from the security business. So I'll start from there. I had the idea to open the club, but I didn't want it to be just any sleazy sex club. We did a lot of research before creating the business we have now. A shitload, actually. Not only did we travel around, touring different clubs that were well established to get an idea of what we wanted for ourselves, but I went to a Dominant training center, also known as The Academy," he explains.

"A Dominant... training center," I repeat, astonished as my mouth gapes. Who knew there was such a thing?

"Yes. Anyone could watch porn or read some shit on the Internet and call themselves a Dom. But you know me, doll. I'm nothing if not thorough. I take my education in any of my endeavors very seriously. I studied under Master Anderson at his academy in Denver. It's a training center for both Dominants and submissives. We studied for several weeks separately, and eventually, under the supervision of our teachers, we practiced scenes together. It also gave us the opportunity, just like any other college, to see what side of BDSM we excelled at, and then we were able to specialize in aspects we wanted to learn more about."

I'm completely fascinated. I have so many questions, and I don't know where to start. "What kinds of specialties were there? What did you pick? How did you find out about The Academy? Why—?"

"Whoa, slow down there," he chuckles. "Let me see. Like, for example, Master Anderson is a Dominant who specializes in the bullwhip. He's trained in everything, but he is known for being the most highly skilled Dom in the world with his bullwhip. The man can split a fucking hair with that thing." He smiles and seems to be thinking back on his teacher fondly. "There was another trainer who came to visit who specialized in kinbaku, which is bondage art. He could tie a submissive up with his special rope and make the knots look like absolutely breathtaking masterpieces. It took great concentration and patience. I'm too squirrely for that, so it didn't really interest me, but it was still beautiful."

"I feel like there's this whole other world right here, within reach, and I had no idea it even existed," I admit, feeling a little overwhelmed but captivated all the same.

"That's how I felt when I first started digging too, doll. But now it's just a part of my life, like it's always been there, as normal to me as stinky cleats to a soccer mom. And you may not realize it, but even in your short amount of time around it, you've grown way more comfortable. On that first day I met you, you could barely look at the stuff on the shelves. But even on your second lesson, you were picking up and handling toys like a champ. It all becomes second nature," he assures, and I beam at his praise.

"So what did you specialize in at your training center?" I ask curiously.

"I was a little different than most of the other students. Yes, there were things I excelled at—I have an uncanny ability to get a submissive to reach subspace more quickly than most—but I actually found I enjoyed the training itself most of all. I respected my teachers so much. They were so knowledgeable and had all of us students hanging on their every word, devouring the information they were giving us. I admired that. I wanted that. It seemed like such a powerful position to be in. So Master Anderson coached me personally in becoming a BDSM instructor myself. And when we opened Club Alias, that was the position I took."

That makes me pause. I hadn't thought about it until he pointed it out, but what would happen now? My heart sinks to the pit of my stomach, making me nauseous. Seth trains the submissives who come into his club. And from what he explained to me during our first two lessons, it's a very hands-on curriculum. I know our relationship is new, but would he expect to keep—

"What's going on in that head of yours, lovely Twyla?" he interrupts my thoughts. "I know that look. Open and honest, remember?" His voice is deep, with just a hint of his commanding tone entering his words.

"I... it just dawned on me that you... you train the submissives at Club Alias." I tuck my hair behind my ear then straighten my glasses nervously.

"Yes, doll. You've known that since the day I met you," he says, glancing between me and the open road.

"Right, but I... what I mean to say is... well... I guess what I'm wondering is..." I blow out a breath in frustration. "Do you, um... plan to continue, uh... doing that for... much longer?" I finally get out, my face heating. I don't do confrontation. And the last thing I want is to cause a fight. I just don't know what being in a relationship with a professional Dominant entails. Discovering that just him mentioning hot sorority girls made me feel overwhelming jealousy, I don't know what I would do if he expected to keep teaching submissives, or more specifically, touching other women.

Suddenly, I feel the car slow and then come to a stop as I see Seth pull us over on the side of the road. My face jerks toward him when I hear him unhook my seatbelt, and before I know what's happening, he pulls me over the center console and into his lap.

"What—"

He slams his lips to mine, cutting off any question I was going ask. His tongue enters my mouth, and the taste of him blankets my consciousness. The way he controls the kiss, like he's mastered every movement of our lips and tongues to draw out the most pleasure, sends my heart into overdrive while the rest of my body melts.

His hand goes to the back of my hair, yanking my head backward until my neck is exposed to his mouth's assault. Beard, teeth, blistering breath—the combination makes me feel wild and completely paralyzed at the same time. God, what this man does to me.

His hot hand lands on my inner thigh before his calloused palm slides upward. His fingers gain access to my wetness, easily through the opening of the loose, comfortable shorts I'm wearing. Slipping his finger beneath the elastic of my panties, he enters me as his teeth skim over the sensitive flesh of my neck, making me suck in a breath between my gritted teeth.

His finger retreats before he thrusts it in again, over and over so deeply he lifts my body with each plunge. He adds a second finger, curling them this time, and I cry out in pleasure. He's not gentle but completely calculated, being rough enough to make it insanely intense but not painful.

"This," he growls against my throat, circling his thumb around my clit, "my beautiful doll, is the last pussy I will ever touch. This," he pulls me to him with the hand still gripping my hair, "is the only body I ever want to feel... see..." Just then, I lose control over all the feelings growing inside me, and I explode, calling out his name as I come from his masterful fingers' assault. And as I pant toward the ceiling of my car, he pulls out of me, and I look down in time see him put his shiny fingers into his mouth before closing his eyes, drawing them out slowly, and finishing his sentence. "...or taste for the rest of my life."

All tension leaves my body, and I collapse against him as I try to catch my breath. He lifts my chin, looking into my eyes as his swirl with intensity.

"I'll still give lessons. I will still be the head trainer of Club Alias. But there are plenty of highly trained Dominant members who will gladly step in to give the hands-on experience. You are the only one, Twyla, who will ever get that from me."

And with that, any doubt hiding in the recesses of my mind disappears.

Thirteen

Seth

W E RAN BY TWYLA'S APARTMENT, letting her change into her work shirt and leggings, and also so she could grab a few things. I informed her she would be staying with me at my loft until everything with Brandon was all taken care of since her sister was safe at Doc's. Judging by the way she didn't put up a fight, I'd say she liked that idea. Little did she know I didn't plan on letting her leave once she settled in. This past week, spending night and day with her, seeing her, touching her, making love to her whenever I wanted... there's no going back after that.

I can't get enough of Twyla Quill. And for the first time, sex is just an added bonus. It's the woman herself I want to submerse myself in. Her intelligence, her dry sense of humor, the way she loves her sister so fiercely, how she protects Astrid, even though

Twyla is the younger of the two. Even the fact she knows none of my movie quotes, because that means I get to be the one to show her the films for the first time. I get to hear her laugh hysterically at the parts that have lost their effect on me because I've seen them so many times, which breathes life into the movies for me once more. It's like getting to watch them for the first time all over again.

And another way I know I fucking love the shit out of her—it doesn't make me mad when she talks during the movie. She asks questions, the backstories of the different Marvel characters, and my chest puffs up with pride as I fill her in on all the details from the comic books. I've never enjoyed talking to a woman as much as I do with her.

She dropped me off at my building on her way to work, promising to come straight back here after her shift ends at midnight. After being gone all week, I've got some work of my own to catch up on. New club membership time is coming up soon; we only open up slots four times a year, because the process is very extensive.

Besides the five-figure membership fee, people are only able to apply if they have a sponsor, someone who is already a member of Club Alias to advocate for their character. Once a thorough background check is complete, the potential member has to go through four therapy sessions with Doc. Our main goal is to provide a safe environment for Dominants and submissives to explore their lifestyle with other people like them. Doc's sessions are an important part of the application process because he is able to weed out the candidates who might have darker intentions. He's able to distinguish if a prospect would be dangerous to our community. There's a fine line between a sexual sadist and a person who actually wants to *hurt* their partner. Besides the Dominant side of the spectrum, Doc can pinpoint submissives with potential triggers. Like in Corbin's wife Vi's case, she was a victim of sexual assault. Without Doc's intensive therapy, it could've been disastrous to give her membership, have her partner up with a Dominant who didn't know her background, and then act out a scene that could make her flashback to her rape. Terrible, irrevocable things can happen to a survivor after a trigger. So it's Doc's duty to keep that from happening.

Wanting to share every part of myself with Twyla and also give her the ability to come into the club whenever she wants, I plan to approach her soon about her going through the application process. She'd get special treatment and not have to pay the fee, of course, but she'd still be required to do the therapy sessions with Doc.

I have a feeling she won't have any problem with the idea. There was no hiding her interest when we talked on the ride home about my training as a Dominant. That and the fact she'd gotten jealous thinking about me being around other women. I'm sure she'd enjoy being able to drop into the club to see what I'm up to. But God as my witness, she'd never find me in any sort of compromising position. I wasn't exaggerating when I told her that hers is the last body I would ever touch. One of the reasons I had never been in a relationship up to this point is because there was no one I desired to be loyal to. There was no one before Twyla who I wanted to put my trust and faith into. Doing that gives a person power, and one thing I never felt willing to do before now was give a woman any type of power over me. But with her, I didn't even question it. Because something told me she would never abuse that control, she'd never use it against me.

Before Twyla, a woman's jealousy would have been a red flag for me, a clinger alert that would have sent me running. Twyla's show of possessiveness made me feel... loved, desired in a way that was much more than sexual. I would never do anything to ruin that. And I would always do anything and everything to protect her heart.

Astrid

"DON'T LOOK AT me like that," I mumble, seeing Scout, Doc's Australian shepherd, watching me as I slip my sneakers on and tie the laces. "I'll be back before your daddy even gets out of his session. I just need a few things from my apartment." I roll my eyes. "Maybe I'll find my sanity while I'm there, seeing how I've now resorted to talking to a damn dog."

I had texted Doc, asking when his appointments would be through for the day. He said an emergency session had been booked and he wouldn't be home until tenish. A new shipment of my products had been delivered to my apartment this morning, and I need to package up a few orders today so Doc can take them to the post office for me in the morning.

I know I should wait for him to take me, but after such a long day at the office, the last thing I want Doc to do is worry about me. He's already done so much for me, while being completely hardheaded about accepting any type of payment for his security services. So instead of asking him to haul me to my apartment this late at night, I'll just run the errand quickly myself. Besides, there's a restraining order in place and a security team keeping an eye on Brandon, so I should be safe if I make this fast.

I toss my cell into my purse and then grab one of the several sets of keys hanging on the wall next to the door, this one with the least fancy emblem on the remote. I'm sneaking off with one of Doc's cars, so the least I can do is not borrow the Audi or the one I can't pronounce. The Chevy truck will work just fine for me, and hopefully he'll never even know I used it. Why one man would need two cars, a truck, and an SUV, I'll never know. But right now, I'm just grateful there's a vehicle for me to drive instead of having to walk to my apartment. I may be able to breathe a little easier now, but I'm not naïve enough to go walking the streets by myself at night, no matter how safe this town claims to be.

I hear Scout whine behind me as I open the door, and I glance back long enough to tell him, "Be a good boy. I'll be right back," before shutting him inside and locking up. I hurry out to the truck, remote in hand, which I use to unlock it before I even reach the tall, black vehicle. Heart pounding, I yank open the door as soon as I grasp the handle, pull myself up into the driver seat, and then slam and lock the door behind me. I start the truck, letting out a nervous laugh and shaking my head.

"Calm the hell down, Astrid," I whisper to myself. "He doesn't know where you are." But even as I say the words, I glance in all the mirrors and then turn around to check the back seat for anyone who might be hiding back there, waiting to attack. Now that I'm outside the fortress that is Doc's house, I feel a lot less confident in making this trip alone. "Ugh!" I growl, frustrated from all the anxiety and paranoia, always having to look over my shoulder because of that bastard. I used to be so fearless, so carefree, and now, no matter where I am or how safe I may be, I always get the eerie sensation that I'm being watched.

Feeling vulnerable, even behind the tinted windows and

locked doors, I put the truck in reverse then make my way out onto the main road. Within minutes, I arrive at my apartment and park in the underground garage. Thankfully, the space right next to the elevator is open. As I turn off the engine, I grab my purse and look around through the windows, trying to see if there's any sign of Brandon hiding between the parked cars.

"You're being paranoid. Just get in quick, grab your shit, and get back to Doc's," I say aloud, now uncaring how crazy I sound talking to not only a dog but to myself as well. The pep talk gives me the courage I need to spring from the truck, slamming the door unnecessarily hard as I bolt to the elevator, rapidly pushing the button over and over, even though I know it won't make it open any faster. I press my back to the wall and face the garage while I wait, my breath coming in short, quick pants as my heart pounds in my ears, my eyes continuously scanning the parking lot. I keep the keys gripped in my hand, wishing I had brought some sort of weapon with me just in case. Being so used to never going anywhere, staying hidden away, I hadn't thought of having to protect myself until this very moment.

Finally, the elevator dings, the sound obscenely loud in the otherwise eerily silent parking garage. I peek inside, seeing the car is empty, and hurry in, pushing the button for my apartment floor. Anxiety fills me when it comes to a stop and the doors slide open. I step forward, leaning just my head out of the elevator to look up and down the hall. And it's not until I see there's not a single soul around that I finally relax. I quickly reach my door, unlock it, slip inside, relock it, and collapse against the smooth surface.

"Jesus fuck," I breathe, feeling completely drained once the tension leaves my body. But I don't give myself very long to enjoy it. "In and out," I remind myself, and I start gathering the short list of things I want to bring with me before I go down to the office to pick up my shipment of makeup.

I go into the bathroom and grab the tampons I'll need soon, knowing full well I'd be mortified if I had to ask the handsome therapist to buy me some at the store. He's kind and easy to talk to, and makes me feel safe in a way I didn't know existed, but asking him to buy my feminine products is more than I could take. Sure, he's an adult, and a doctor no less, but it seems like that's something really intimate to ask a man for, something only a wife would ask her husband to do for her, and only if her husband was a special kind of guy.

Brandon had most certainly not been that kind of guy. My period every month was the only week I got any sort of peace. He wouldn't even make me sleep next to him during those blissful five days, the mere thought of the blood disgusting him.

I shake myself out of the memory, leaning over the tub to grab my bottle of body wash. And that's when I hear it.

Rattling.

What is that? The subtle sound of metal against metal coming from the living room. Almost like a key entering a lock, but not. More like scratching and tapping.

My heart pounds in my ears, nearly blocking out the noise as I slowly peek out of the bathroom toward the front door. And to my horror, I see where the sound is coming from as it ends with a click, the knob turns, and the door slowly opens.

Twyla

What did you think while you were reading Vi's book? :smiling devil:

I giggle, reading the text message Seth sent me. It's been pretty slow tonight at work, so I've been passing the time chatting back and forth with him as he catches up on work at the club. I had sent my sister a text earlier asking if she needed me to bring her anything on my way home, but seeing as it's almost 11:00 p.m., she's probably already asleep. I'm closing tonight, so I've got an hour left of my shift.

I reply to Seth's message, heat filling my core as I answer his question.

Me: Knowing it was you who'd explained all the kinky stuff in the story, I wondered what it would be like to experience what the characters were doing.

His reply is almost immediate, as they always are.

Seth: Reeeally? *wiggles eyebrows* Any part in particular get you wet, doll?

His naughty question makes my face flame, not only because of what he's asking but because there certainly was one scene that stood out in my mind. And now I'll have to be open and honest with my answer.

I start to type out my response, but the bell over the door rings as a customer comes inside, so I hurry to reply.

Me: I'd like to try... Hold that thought. Customer.

I feel my phone buzz as I slide it into my back pocket, but don't look at it as I come out from behind the counter to help the shopper.

I walk around the tall revolving tower of nipple pasties, trying to spot the person who had come in, and find the dark-haired man standing and facing the wall of women's lingerie.

Ah, an easy one, I think. I've had quite a few men come in looking for something sexy for their significant other to wear for them. I find it quite endearing, the boyfriend or husband taking the time to put thought into their selection, and it's always interesting to see which outfit they pick. You'd think they'd all go for the naughty leather numbers, with scraps of fabric that do nothing to save anything for the imagination. But on the contrary, a lot of them have been picking pretty things, lacy panties and soft teddies in whites and pinks, items that would give their girlfriend or wife a very innocent look.

"Welcome to Toys for Twats. Can I help you find anything?" I ask as I approach.

"As a matter of fact, Twy, you can."

The moment his deep voice fills the silence, my heart plummets to the floor. Brandon turns to face me, and suddenly the side of my head explodes with pain just before the rest of my body falls to meet my heart, and the store goes black.

Fourteen

Astrid

AS THE TALL MALE FIGURE COMES through the door, I take a deep breath to let out a blood-curdling scream but swallow it as soon as I see Doc's handsome face in the lamp's light. I grow lightheaded at the roller coaster of adrenaline and relief, emptying my lungs as I collapse against the bathroom's doorframe.

"Jesus H., Doc. What the hell are you doing here? And how the fuck did you get in? I definitely locked the door behind me!" I squawk breathlessly as I sink down to the floor, plopping onto my ass like a deflated balloon. My heart feels like it's beating a mile a minute.

He strolls forward until he towers over me, his bearded jaw set as he pulls a thin pair of tools from his pocket, wiggling them between his fingers before replacing them where they were.

"Four seconds, goddess," he growls, using the name he's been calling me the last few days. The endearment warms my heart while his tone makes my blood run cold—a very strange feeling. "I opened your locked door in four... seconds."

"You're a man of many talents," I murmur, trying to shake off the way his mesmerizing eyes penetrate me with his disappointment. "How did you—"

"There are sensors on all of the doors and windows of my home. The moment you opened the front door, I watched you steal my truck on my surveillance app on my phone," he tells me, and I instantly feel a pang of guilt. "When you disappeared from my cameras' view as you pulled out of my driveway, I tracked you with the GPS I have in all of my vehicles. I was already on my way home, and pulled into your garage not even a full two minutes after you had parked."

I roll my eyes. "Hell, I'm surprised you don't have a Go-Pro attached to your dog," I gripe, swatting my hair out of my face, beginning to squirm under his laser-like stare.

"Micro-camera. In his collar," he states.

"You've gotta be shitting me." My eyes widen.

"Scout is a highly trained retired military working dog. And he can obviously follow orders to stay the hell put a fuck of a lot better than someone else I know." His nostrils flare.

Rage fills me at that. "One, I'm not a dog." I clamber to my feet, straightening my tank with haughty movements. His eyes drop to my breasts and then meet my eyes again so quickly I question whether it actually happened. Either way, his intense expression never wanes. "And two, you have no right to *order* me to do anything. I'm a grown-ass wo—"

His mouth slams down on mine so ferociously my body bows,

and if it weren't for his massive arm circling me, I would have fallen backward. He's so fucking tall my face aims toward the ceiling as he devours my lips, and finally, as my mind catches up to put all of these different puzzle pieces together to realize he's kissing me, I whimper and go dead weight when his tongue plunges into my mouth. He holds me to him effortlessly, his whole body wrapping around me like a cocoon. And while I feel so tiny, so helpless in the arms of such a giant man, even as he takes his anger at my insubordination out on my lips, I feel nothing but safe. Well... that and completely turned on in a way I never thought possible.

Just as my hands find his shoulders and run upward, over his neck and into the back of his short hair, his phone rings loudly, the sound echoing off the bathroom walls.

He growls as he breaks the kiss, leaving me panting against his chest as he pulls his cell out of his pocket.

"Seth?" It comes out as a bark, and he clears his throat. I look up to see the frustrated look melt from his face as it's replaced by worry, before a serious mask locks into place while he listens to Seth speak.

Doc's eyes find mine, his focus shifting back and forth between my irises.

"Stay calm. We're on our way," he says, hanging up and grabbing my hand.

"What's wrong?" I ask quietly, dread filling me.

"Brandon's taken Twyla. Let's go."

Seth

Fifteen minutes pass without a response to my last text message to Twyla. And then twenty, then thirty. By then, I've sent her a few more, still with no reply. It's still a half hour before the store closed, so maybe she had more customers come in, but something in my gut tells me not to blow her silence off. I call her work number just in case her cell has died, and when she doesn't answer that, I know something is very, very wrong.

I log into the surveillance system, and with a few keystrokes, I tap into the cameras outside Toys for Twats. Seeing Twyla's car still in the parking lot, my brow furrows. Why wouldn't she be answering either of her phones? Have my messages asking her about her thoughts on trying BDSM freaked her out so badly she's ignoring me? Surely not. Not after seeing the heat in her eyes while we were talking about it in the car less than eight hours ago.

I switch the view to the cameras Bryan had put outside Brandon's hotel when he went to serve him the restraining order. And when I see his car isn't in the lot, where it's been the whole time since the camera was installed, my heart pounds inside my chest.

I pull up our GPS program, scanning the map for any signs of Brandon's whereabouts. To ensure he was driving back to California, Bryan had also placed a microscopic tracking device beneath his car. But when I locate the dot on the screen indicating Brandon's movements, he's not heading south on I-95 to catch I-10 to head toward the west coast. No, he's heading east, and when I rewind his tracker to see where he's been, that's when I see the dot had stopped at Twyla's work for a total of six minutes.

With my heartbeat now pounding in my ears, I go back into the surveillance program and type in the time for the footage from the store's parking lot camera. And I can't explain the emotion that comes over me when I see the motherfucker carrying an unconscious Twyla out to his car before speeding out onto the street and out of sight.

I grab my cell, my hands shaking as I call Doc. He picks up on the first ring, his voice coming out gruff. "Seth?"

"Doc, he's... he's fucking got my woman. Brandon took her. I've been trying to get a hold of her for half an hour, and when she wouldn't answer, I tracked Brandon. He left the store twenty-four minutes ago, heading east," I tell him all in one breath, rage and panic filling me in equal parts as I say it out loud.

"Stay calm. We're on our way," Doc replies, and I let out a maniacal short burst of laughter.

"Stay calm?" I shout, but he already hung up.

How the fuck he expects me to stay calm when—

I'm so angry at myself I would pay someone to beat my ass right now. How fucking stupid had I been? All our focus had been on keeping Astrid safe, keeping her hidden in a place where Brandon didn't know her location. With the restraining order served and surveillance on him in place, we thought we were still being extra cautious by not letting Astrid out in the open until he had left. We all thought it was her we needed to keep safe, his obsession with *her*, not Twyla.

He must've grown frustrated, unable to get to his ex-girlfriend. And now he's going to take it out on my woman.

I jump up from my computer chair, my hands diving into my

hair. "Fuck!" I growl, as I try to think of what to do next, and just then, Corbin and Bryan storm into my office.

"Doc called. What's the plan?" Bryan demands, coming to stand in front of my desk, his arms crossing over his wide chest.

My brain's jumbled. I've never been so angry or scared in my entire life. "I... I don't know. I can't think straight!"

Corbin comes around my desk and grips onto my shoulders, giving me a jerk to force my eyes to his. "We're going to get her back, brother. She'll be all right. But right now, we need to know details, and we need to make a plan," he says calmly, and the sureness in his expression makes me snap out of my panic.

I run down everything I've seen from the cameras and the GPS, and soon, Doc shows up with Astrid, her face showing the same terror I feel on the inside, knowing her abusive asshole of an ex now has Twyla.

Finalizing our plans, everyone splits. Doc will be at the club, making sure everything runs smoothly here and to keep an eye on Astrid. She threw a fit when we told her she couldn't come with us to get her sister, but Doc was able to settle her down, and finally she understood if we wanted to get Twyla back safely, we couldn't worry about her too.

Corbin and Bryan run to their offices, grabbing whatever gear they choose to bring with us, and I scoop up my laptop, feeling utterly useless as the other two men return, sliding their handguns into holsters beneath their jackets.

"Wipe that look off your face, man. We're just the muscle. Your brain makes our job easy. If it weren't for you, we wouldn't know where she is. Now let's go get her back," Corbin grunts, and I let out a breath, following them out of my office.

Fifteen

Twyla

I GROAN THE SECOND I GAIN consciousness, bringing a splitting headache along with it. My brain throbs inside my skull, and as I try to blink my eyes open, I can't focus. My vision is blurred, and I realize I'm not wearing my glasses. But even without them, I can usually see better than this.

I go to reach for the side of my head where I vaguely remember being hit, but my arm doesn't move. I tilt my face to the side to see my wrist, and barely make out the shackle there. The sound of metal clanging as I jerk at it helps me distinguish what's keeping it in place.

My heart pounds, realizing I can't move as I pull at my feet and my other hand. And when I look down my body, only seeing the hazy outline of my light skin, it takes everything in me to keep down my nausea. I am completely naked. *Completely* naked, and strapped down to some kind of table.

"Who knew that's what I'd find under the clothes of that cunt's mousy little sister?"

Brandon's voice fills me with dread. How did this even happen?

"Wh—"

"Shut up, bitch!" he shouts, and I scream as something stings the side of my ribs. I glance down, but all I can make out is a glowing blue light as tears fill my eyes.

"Awww, what's the matter, Twy? I thought you were into all this kinky shit. Isn't that why you work at a sex shop now?" he taunts, bringing the blue light closer to my face. I press my head back against the hard surface I'm lying on, and squeeze my eyes tightly as the light grows uncomfortably bright. "Isn't that why you go to your little boyfriend's sex club?"

The light is suddenly gone, and I open my eyes, even though they're basically useless. I listen for his movements, trying to figure out where he is and what he's up to. When he appears once again as a dark blob next to me, I can't hold back my sob. And suddenly, my whole chest explodes with pain as he hits me with some type of leather whip with a bunch of tails. I've seen them in my shop, but since Seth hasn't taught me about them yet and a customer hasn't inquired about them, I have no idea what they're for. Surely it's not for this purpose. *No one could find this pleasurable,* I think, and then cry out as he strikes me with it once again across my naked breasts.

"What? You don't like being flogged? Hmm... must run in the family. Your sister didn't like being beat much either, but she sure did ask for it a lot," he sneers. "Thought you might like it though since you go to a BDSM club and all. That's why I brought you here, Twy. It may not be as nice and upscale as your nerdy little fuck's place, but it works. They didn't even bat an eye when I carried you in here. Thought we were roleplaying or some shit. Even opened the door for me when I asked for one of the private rooms."

He laughs evilly, making my skin crawl at the image he paints. I try not to think of him undressing me, touching me as he locked my limbs down to the table, but I fail, and it sends me into a panic at what he might do to me now that I'm at his mercy. I suck in a lungful of air and scream at the top of my lungs, yanking at the shackles as hard as I can, hoping someone will come in to see what's happening. But as I run out of breath and my limbs grow weak from my struggle, I cringe as Brandon laughs harder.

"No one's coming to help you, Twy. They've got the music so loud out there. You can barely hear it in here, so I'm assuming these rooms are sound proof. That, and I bet they're used to hearing people scream all the time. Good try though." He strikes me once again across my chest, and then at the top of my thighs, the leather straps like razor blades on my soft flesh. I've never in my life felt something so painful, and I burst into tears as he hits me once again. "Oh, poor little Twyla. Your fuckboy must be taking it easy on you if you're already crying. I have to admit, though, now I've gotten a taste of these different toys, I kind of regret not taking your sister up on her offer when she asked me to spice things up in the bedroom. I should practice a few more on you, see which ones I like best, so when I get Astrid to come back home with me, I'll know how to use them properly."

The thought of him coming anywhere near Astrid sends me into hysterics. I've heard so many horror stories of women leaving abusive relationships, only to go back to the person who brainwashed them enough to make them believe they can't live without them. I cry and thrash on the table, trying my best to get my hands loose, but nothing works.

He leans over me, his breath smelling of liquor as he growls in my face, "Sucks to have something taken from you, doesn't it? You took Astrid from me, so now I've taken your freedom, and I'll steal her back too. You hurt me, and I swear you won't leave here until I've hurt you in return."

I swallow painfully, my mouth completely dry. "What?" I wheeze, my eyes clamping shut as I brace myself when his arm raises over his head. I hear the flogger slice through the air before the tails burn the skin of my stomach.

"Oh, you haven't figured it out yet? I thought you were supposed to be the smart sister." His voice sounds like pure evil. "I could've gotten to Astrid at any time. You left her alone plenty of times when you were interviewing for jobs, running errands, and then while you were at work or out fucking the guy you just met. I must say, Twy—that was really surprising. And here I thought all these years that you were a prude with a stick shoved up your ass. Little did I know you prefer something different up there. Anal beads? A butt plug, maybe? Or did you just go straight for your little Dom's cock? Hmm?"

He must see the surprise in my eyes through my tears, pain, and terror, because he continues his taunting. "Oh, yeah. I know what he is. A little inquiring about becoming a member of what I thought was a nightclub you were working at, and it was easy to get the owner's name and the fact he was a Dominant. Who the fuck names their kid Seven anyway?"

I don't let him see my relief when I realize he hasn't somehow found out Seth's real name. That information in a person like Brandon's hands could've been disastrous. If he released that publicly, all the hard work Seth put into keeping people's identities secret—how many members would lose faith in his abilities and leave the club for fear theirs would be leaked too?

"So what are you still doing here?" My voice cracks as I tremble, my body completely rigid from the pain across my front.

"She was mine!" he yells in my face, making me flinch. He rears his arm back, once more bringing down the flogger with all his strength across my hips. I sob, yanking at the shackles as the pain bursts through me like wildfire. "You came in the middle of the night and took her from me! And now you're going to be punished for it." He whips me again, and this time, my skin starts to go numb.

Seeing I don't react as intensely, he disappears for a moment, and the amount of fear inside me doubles, not knowing what he will bring when he returns.

Seth

"HE'S HAD ALMOST an hour's head start on us. Do you know what he could have done to her in an hour?" I murmur, fidgeting in the passenger seat of Corbin's SUV.

"But he was driving for half of that hour, bro. Not much he could've done while he was driving. We don't know what he wants with her. The only thing I've come up with is maybe he's going to try to make a trade, Twyla for Astrid. He has no idea we have a tracking device on him," Corbin tells me, going for reassurance, but all I can think about is what Brandon could've done in that second half hour.

"No guns in his name. No weapons in his car. No weapons in his hotel room," Bryan says in his monotone way, and I look at him over my shoulder. His face is serious, and he meets my eye. "Checked when he was eating at the diner next to the hotel two days ago."

I nod, feeling somewhat better.

"What have you found out about this address he stopped at, Seth? We're ten minutes out," Corbin warns, and I feel a surge of adrenaline.

I look down at my laptop, checking the screen. The results are finally up. "Something called The Red Rocket. One-star rating on Google." I pause to read a review. "'Skeezy sex club with cheap drinks,' says one person. 'Scared we were going to catch something the second we walked in,' says another." My hands shoot to my skull, dragging through my hair in frustration. "This is where the fucker took my woman. And has been there with her for thirty goddamn minutes." The tiny bit of relief I'd felt only moments ago completely disappears.

"Been there. Place is a shithole. Been through four different owners in as many years. Drinks are cheap, probably in an attempt to dull how disgusting the place is," Bryan chips in.

"Fuck," I growl. "What's the plan once we get there again? I can't fucking think."

"We get there, find her, we'll detain him while you get her out, and then we call the cops. Easy," Corbin replies.

"Okay. I just need to see she's all right. That's all I want right now. She's... she's the only thing that matters." My voice cracks, but I don't give a fuck that my best friends can see my emotions. Corbin especially. He'd been through something with Vi that sent him into a rage so bad the guy who assaulted her ended up with a missing appendage.

Seeing the sign for The Red Rocket up ahead, I address the guys, "Before we get in there, I just wanted to thank you two for having my back. I... I'm the tech guy behind our jobs. You're the ones who put your lives at risk every day. I fight with my brain. It's the only thing I know how to do. I've never been in a fight. I'm... I'm not a violent person. You know this. And the pictures she showed me of what this asshole did to her sister... I'm just glad you're here."

"Always, brother," Corbin says low, and Bryan grunts his agreement from the back seat.

That's all the talking we have time for before we turn into the parking lot of the rundown building and come to a halt. We jump out of the SUV and make our way to the door, as I follow them scanning the parking lot for Brandon's car. Spotting it a few vehicles down from the front entrance, my heart pummels my ribcage, seeing it in person for the first time after only seeing it in the surveillance footage up until now. It suddenly makes this all the more real. This is really happening. This motherfucker had knocked Twyla out, kidnapped her, and brought her to this shithole. He had taken the woman I love, and now he will pay.

Corbin yanks open the blacked-out door, a poor mimicry of the one at Club Alias, and as we step inside, we're immediately blocked by two men, both over six feet tall and almost as wide as we're bombarded by loud music, heavy with bass.

"No men allowed. Only couples and women," one of them states, his arms crossing over his chest.

Corbin steps forward, and the two dark men spread their feet in unison, ready to block his path. "We're here for a friend. She's been brought here against her will. Step aside, and we'll get her and be on our way," he tells them calmly over the music, but they instantly go on the offense, stepping forward.

"No one's come in that looked like they weren't here to have a good time. Now run along," the one on the right says, clearly not giving a shit that there might be a woman in the building getting—

No. I can't think about that. And right as I open my mouth to try to reason with the two people standing in the way of me getting to Twyla, all hell breaks loose as Corbin and Bryan lunge at the exact same time, fists and elbows flying in all directions. As the four men grunt, landing punches and cursing at each other, Bryan yells, "Go!" in my direction, and I instantly spring into action.

I leap over a body, not taking the time to see who it is as I take in the club. Disgusting red vinyl couches line one wall, with cheap tables in between. There are several couples having sex, but I barely take in specifics of their positions as I search for just one face. Just my Twyla. And none of these people are her.

My eyes scan the bar area, but all that's there is a man bending a woman over one of the stools, the bartender in front of them looking bored or stoned, or maybe both. Wherever Twyla is, she's not in this main room.

I storm toward the back, where three black doors line the wall. I jerk at the first knob, but it doesn't budge. With adrenaline pumping through me, and fear for Twyla's safety growing the longer she's alone with the fucktard who took her, I rear back and kick in the door, the cheap wood shattering as it bounces off the wall.

The woman being fucked against a makeshift cross screams as her partner falls backward, covering his dick as he scoots away on his ass. "What the fuck, man?" he yells at me, but I don't even think to apologize as I move to the next room.

Again, locked. My hands shake with rage as sweat pours down my temples. As time passes without my eyes on Twyla, unable to see she's safe, the tighter something twists inside me. And when I kick in the door, it takes a moment to register what I see before me.

I finally find my woman. But she's nearly unrecognizable in her agony. The bulky, dark-haired man holds a violet wand to the tender flesh of her ribs, burning her as his other arm halts midair before he can hit the already bloody skin of her thighs with the metal-tipped whip in his hand. Her eyes open as she continues to sob, her tear-soaked face turning more toward the smashed door.

I can't tell if she recognizes it's me or not because her glasses are missing and her eyes are bloodshot, but at her whimpered, "Help me... please," whatever it was that was tightening inside me before reaches its threshold and snaps.

I charge Brandon like a bull seeing nothing but red, making it to him in three strides and so fast he doesn't even have time to lift the violet wand from Twyla's blistered skin. My fist connects with his face at the same moment I grab the electric device with my other hand, yanking it away from her flesh. The blue light immediately goes out, but the rage inside me sparks anew when I see what he's done to her up close. As he lunges toward me, having regained his footing, I rear back with the wand, smashing the glass across the front of his skull.

Never in my life have I ever wanted to kill someone with my own hands. But that's exactly what I have in mind as I wrap the cord of the device around his neck, maneuvering my body around his until I'm at his back. As he struggles for breath, I wrap the ends of the cord around my hands so it won't slip and use all my adrenaline-fueled strength to pull it as tight as I can around his throat. Visions of slicing his head clean off fill my mind, my lip lifting in a snarl as I growl, "You fucking sorry-ass piece of shit. You got off on beating the fuck out of her sister, and then dared to draw blood on my woman? I will fucking kill you, motherfucker."

Brandon tries to defend himself from behind, throwing his elbow back as he claws at the cord around his neck, but I dodge it easily. Everything above the white cable turns purple from lack of oxygen, and something inside me wants to laugh maniacally as I feel him begin to weaken. I glance down into Twyla's face, seeing she now recognizes me since she heard my voice. But it's not relief I find there. It's growing panic.

"I'm here, doll. No one will ever hurt you ever again. I'm here," I say, making my voice as gentle as I can, all while choking the life out of the cocksucker who did this to her.

"Se— Seven. You have to stop. You have to stop, please," she whimpers, and my brow furrows in confusion. Why is she calling me by my Dom name? And more importantly, why is she telling me to let Brandon go?

"You have to, baby. Life for a life, remember? I'm alive. You saved me. So you've gotta stop. Please," she begs, but no matter how much her eyes plead with me to do as she asks, my hands just won't let go. Especially as I glance down her naked, shackled body, seeing the bloody stripes he has left all over her perfect skin.

In fact, my grip tightens even more as I see the burn on her ribs, knowing it will scar and be there for the rest of her life if I don't kill this motherfucker soon and get her to the hospital fast enough. No way will I let this piece of shit brand the love of my life, leaving his mark for her to remember this nightmare every time she looks in the mirror. No, I need to make him die faster.

But as I lift my leg to press my knee into the middle of his back for leverage, I'm tackled from the side. With my hands wrapped securely around the cord, it jerks Brandon along with us, and he falls to the ground. The awkward position of my arms makes them feel like they're going to pop out of their joints at any moment, and I finally let go, ready to lunge and beat the fuck out of him as he tries to catch his breath. But Corbin's voice enters my consciousness.

"Take care of your woman. We've got him."

The mention of Twyla clears the rage-induced fog, remembering she's strapped to a table, naked and in excruciating pain. I spin away from the men as I search for the key to the shackles, finding it immediately on a table full of instruments I pray he hasn't had time to use on her. I hurry to the foot of the table, unlocking her ankles before circling to the head to open the ones around her wrists. She cries out as she tries to lift her arms, and the sound of her agony makes me want to go back to strangling the life out of the fucker who did this to her. But instead, I scoop her into my arms as carefully as I can, murmuring a thank-you to Bryan as he quickly wraps a towel around her body before I carry her out of the room.

With her in my arms, I cease thinking about Brandon, knowing my partners will take care of him.

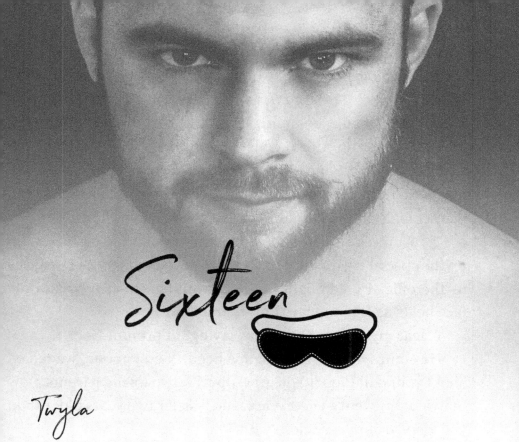

Sixteen

Twyla

Six weeks later

"I'T'S YOUR FOURTH SESSION WITH ME, Twyla," Doc states from his leather chair across from where I sit on the matching sofa in his office. "The first thing I always do with all prospective members of Club Alias during this last appointment is go over everything we've learned throughout our time together."

"Sounds good to me, Doc," I reply, watching him pull his ever-present notepad off his side table and into his lap.

"This'll be a first for me though because I've never had someone's partner join us for one of my sessions before," he adds, sending a small smile in Seth's direction, where he's lounging on the cushion next to me.

"Saves time, bro. Now I won't have to waste an hour watching the video since I'll be here to hear everything in person. You know what I could be doing with that extra hour?" Seth asks, turning to me and wiggling his eyebrows.

I roll my eyes and swat his chest. "Behave. This is serious business. I want to be treated exactly like every other member of your club. No special treatment just because I live there."

"Trust me, doll. The submissives at the club can't even dream up the special treatment I'm gonna give you as soon as Doc gives us the official green light," Seth murmurs seductively, and my face heats as Doc watches our interaction.

I clear my throat. "You were saying?" I prompt Doc.

He smiles faintly, shaking his head. "Session one, we talked about your childhood. You grew up with two loving parents, now married for twenty-eight years, and a sister two years older than you who you are very close with."

I watch him closely, trying to see any change in expression when he talks about Astrid, but he's damn good. The man has a professional poker face that could rival Seth's. The only thing I notice is his eyes soften a bit at the mention of my sister.

"Session two, we talked about your high school and college years, and your professional career as a chemical engineer. Another first for me when initiating a member into Club Alias: you were a virgin until recently, so there was no sexual history for us to cover during this session. This is normally when a prospect and I delve into the reasons they are drawn to the BDSM lifestyle, but in your case, the reason is currently ogling you and giving me the overwhelming urge to disinfect my couch," Doc grumbles.

I could feel Seth staring at me for the past minute, but I had locked eyes on Doc as he spoke, doing my damnedest to ignore my goofy-ass boyfriend. Now, I squint my eyes and turn my glare on him, immediately dropping the mock expression of anger and bursting into laughter when I see what he's doing. He runs his fingertip around the inside of his plump lips, flicking his tongue raunchily as he stares me straight in the eye. Now that he's got my attention, he grinds his hips as he continues whatever he's doing to his mouth, the movement accentuated by his camo fanny pack. One of thirteen in all different colors I discovered when I moved in with him two weeks ago.

"What in the world is wrong with you, Seth?" I giggle. "This is serious!"

"I don't know, doll. Doc said virgin, and all of a sudden I wanted to take this dee-yock"—he humps the air, making the fanny pack bounce—"and put it in yo' vag. We need to hurry this up, 'cause I'm fixin's to fuck ya."

I slap my hand over his mouth in an attempt to get him to stop, but he just licks my palm, and I pull it away to wipe on my denim-covered thigh. "I'm sorry, Doc," I tell him, trying to keep a straight face.

"Uh-uh, lovely Twyla. You know the rules. Name the movie. You have to name the movie when it's one I've made you watch... or a good spanking is in order." He says the last part with a British accent after reminding me of the game we've been playing for over a month.

I groan, giving in because I know he won't stop until I do. "*Wanderlust*. And the spanking reference is from *Bedazzled*."

"God, I'm so hot for you right n—"

"Seth!"

"Fine. I'll be thinking of your reward for getting the bonus movie." He settles back against the cushion.

When I look at Doc again, ready to apologize once more, I'm surprised to find there's not a spec of annoyance on his face. His eyes are laughing, and the corner of his lips is turned up as he looks to Seth and me. He seems to nod to himself, and then picks up where he left off.

"Session three was different than the others. In depth, we went over recent events that could've had lasting damage on your feelings about the BDSM lifestyle. You got emotional talking about the things that had gone through your mind while held against your will," Doc says gently, and Seth reaches over and takes my hand. When I look at him, his face is sober.

"You are a very strong woman, Twyla," Doc continues. "And remarkably selfless. In the middle of being hurt, it was fear you felt over Brandon taking Astrid back that scared you the most. And after nearly half an hour of physical torture, when Seth came in and rescued you, you still had the mind to call him by his Dom name, Seven, so your attacker wouldn't learn his identity, keeping him and his business safe from that information getting out. These things added to the fact you had quit your job in California and moved across the country in order to help your sister escape an abusive relationship... you are quite an extraordinary person."

My face heats at the praise. It feels weird getting kudos for just being who I am as a person. "Thanks, Doc," I murmur, feeling Seth squeeze my hand. "I mean, I think I got pretty lucky. It could've been way worse. Yeah, it sucked being knocked out and beaten to hell for half an hour, but at least he didn't... um, yeah. Thank you."

"While you shouldn't minimize what happened to you— no one should ever have to go through being kidnapped and physically harmed—you're also very right. It could have been much worse. And thankfully it wasn't, which is why I believe you've bounced back pretty quickly," he agrees, and I nod. "Also in our last session, you confided you couldn't understand how Seth could love you so instantaneously, even though you felt the same way about him in the same short amount of time. I hope you can now see why a person like him, one who had been used and taken advantage of for so many years, could be so drawn to a genuinely selfless, caring woman such as yourself."

I shift in my seat, embarrassed over Doc talking about that in front of Seth, even though I know all three of the other partners of Club Alias besides Doc would be privy to videos of our sessions. It's part of the rules for membership so they would know all their members' pasts as a safety precaution during business hours.

Seth lifts my hand to his lips, speaking over my knuckles in that sweet way he does. "I love you for many more reasons than that, lovely Twyla, but your beautiful, generous soul is one of my favorite things about you."

My heart swells inside my chest, and I get choked up, tears springing to my eyes. It never fails to shock me whenever he so openly expresses his feelings, especially when it's in front of his friends.

"Another one being dat ass," he adds, making me snort.

He's always good about adding just enough humor when things get serious, a facet both my sister and Doc think is a reason why Seth and I fit so perfectly. He brightens up my once dull, regimented life, while I've given him someone to trust in, who gets to see deeper than just his sexy and funny exterior. I understand his intellectual side where most people don't, allowing him to open up to me about more than sex and pop culture.

"So for the rest of the session, I'd like to talk about where you two see yourselves fitting in to our BDSM community. Twyla, you have shown classic character traits of a submissive, which pairs perfectly with Seth's dominance. But you also bring out a side of him he's never explored before—making love, being intimate with emotions involved. And from what both of you have told me in separate sessions, that side of your sexual relationship has been flawless," Doc says.

I look over at Seth, a smile tugging at my lips. I feel ridiculously giddy over the fact he had told his friend he enjoyed having sex with me, even though I knew from the frequency in which he wanted to make love to me that he couldn't be hating it. He gives me his evil grin, making my core clench.

"Twyla, having never practiced a D/s relationship before, how do you see BDSM playing a part in your life?" Doc asks.

"Well, I've done some research, and I know there are couples who live the lifestyle 24/7. I don't really see that as something I would enjoy, so I would definitely lean toward the other side of the spectrum, our D/s relationship being only in our sex life. And not all the time then either. I very much love the vanilla sex we have, which feels weird calling it that because there's nothing plain and boring about it. But I want to learn to be a proper submissive for the evenings I spend with him at the club," I explain, and side-eye Seth when his arm shoots into the air.

"Ooo, pick me, pick me!" he chants, and Doc lifts a brow at him.

"Is there something you'd like to add, Seth?" he asks sarcastically.

"Yus!" Seth says victoriously. "I have an idea, Doc. Tell me if you think it'd work. Okay, what if we save the BDSM part of our relationship only for the club. That way there is a clear line there. Unless, of course, we both wanted to explore it elsewhere."

Doc nods thoughtfully. "That could work. And like any scene, if you'd want to act one out somewhere outside the club, you'd discuss it in detail first. But it would be good to establish that whenever the two of you are inside Club Alias, you are Twyla's Dom and she is your sub. It's still very important that she calls you Seven there, and making it a rule that you are in your D/s personas while you are at the club will make it easier to not slip up. Twyla, would you agree to this?"

"Definitely," I state. "When he asked me to consider becoming a member, that's what I had expected anyway. Seth *is* a Dominant. That's part of him as a person. That's who he is when he is at Club Alias, and I understand in order to share my life with him, I'll be his submissive while we're there. Happily. Very, *very* happily. I'm excited about learning everything Seven, the Master, has to teach me, and much more than just sex toys."

Suddenly, I'm yanked across the couch and find myself in Seth's lap, and before I can scold him for interrupting my therapy session yet again, his lips are on mine, and I forget all about what we were talking about.

But the kiss ends as swiftly as it began, and I'm transferred back to my spot on the couch, with Seth's arm across my lap, his big hand wrapping around my knee in a sweet show of possession.

"Well, now that all of that is established, there's one last thing I'd like to discuss. And it's actually a good thing Seth is here so we can hear his input," Doc tells us as if nothing happened.

"Okay," I prompt, suddenly nervous about what he might say because of the serious look on his face.

"Twyla, what Brandon did to you in that place, I want you

to understand that never would have happened at Club Alias." Doc's tone is imploring, and my pulse quickens at this change in subject. "We have strict rules at our establishment. The Dom's there are all highly trained in the devices and equipment we have in our playrooms. In order for a Dom to even be allowed into one of the different themed rooms is if he has been certified in all the things that room has to offer. We have security and documentation in place to ensure a Dom who isn't trained in, say, a violet wand, will never be allowed in the playroom that holds that specific device. This keeps the submissives from being hurt by someone who doesn't know what they're doing. Also, another reason that never would've happened at our club is because our playrooms do not have locking doors. There are curtains that can be closed for privacy, but even so, there are also security cameras inside each room. We take every precaution to make sure Club Alias is a safe place for people to explore their alternate lifestyle."

"That's very reassuring. Thank you, Doc." I look over at Seth. "I might have to get used to the idea of people being able to watch us while we're using a playroom though."

He squeezes my knee. "This is where you could apply your special treatment card I was trying to give you, doll. Perk of being the owner's woman. If you don't want anyone watching what we do behind the closed curtain, my partners will respect your wishes. But you'd be surprised what a rush it can be acting out a scene in front of an audience. They are not there to judge. The good thing about such a strict membership process is we've established a group of like-minded people with a passion for what we do. They see nothing but beauty in the scenes, the bodies and actions like living art. So if you ever wanted to try that, it's always an option later on, when you're more comfortable."

My eyes have gone half-mast listening to Seth's deep voice talking so passionately about his club. The way he spoke made it sound sensual and invigorating, instead of dark and potentially humiliating.

He reaches up and pushes my glasses up my nose before running his fingertip down the bridge, something he does when he just wants to touch me in any way he can.

"Now that we've made that clear, Twyla," Doc says low, as if trying not to break the trance Seth has lulled me into, "I wanted to suggest your Dom acting out a scene with you. Specifically one incorporating the tools and device that were used on you at the other club."

That gets my attention, and I reach for Seth, wrapping my hand around his thick bicep for comfort. "I...." I don't really know how to respond to that. The objects Brandon had used on me were terrible, painful things that I saw no way they could ever be pleasurable.

"The man by your side, the one you have given your heart to, put your trust into, the one who rescued you from the person who hurt you so badly... he is a Master in every single item at our club. He trained at one of the most highly respected schools for Dominants in the country, if not the world. I believe it would be very beneficial for your healing if you would allow *Seven* to demonstrate the way those tools are *meant* to be used—to bring pleasure," Doc explains, and goose bumps rise on my flesh as he uses Seth's Dom name. There's power in it, and nothing but true respect in Doc's words. It's easy to forget how impressive the Seven side is when I'm so used to only being around my sweet Seth.

My Seth. I trust him with my life. So I should have no problem trusting him with my body. I've given myself to him over and over, letting him take me to heights I never thought possible. And that's with him making love to me, something he'd never done with another person before, making him unpracticed in a way. I can only imagine what he could make me feel by using skills he had mastered.

"It would be at the club?" I ask to confirm.

"Yes, and you can choose what would make you more comfortable—just you and me, or we could have Doc there or watching through the security camera. You can also choose whether it's just a demonstration of the tools, or if you'd want it to continue into something more. All up to you, doll," Seth tells me.

I nibble at the inside of my cheek, thinking it through, and then finally come to a decision. "Okay. I'd like for it to start out as just a demonstration, with Doc observing behind the camera just in case I freak out and you need backup. If it turns into something more, you give him a signal, and the camera shuts off. I don't think I'm ready to be an exhibitionist just yet."

"Deal," Seth agrees.

Doc nods. "In that case, I officially clear you for membership at Club Alias."

I smile nervously as Seth whoops and does a fist pump into the air. "Shake and bake, baby," he says in a thick southern accent, rubbing his hands together.

And even though I'm anxious as hell, I'm also pretty excited, so to assure him I'm really in this for the long haul, I lean over and kiss his cheek, whispering, *"Talladega Nights."*

He pulls me to him, tickling my ribs and making me squeal. "I'll take care of you, Twy. But we might as well go ahead and set up our signal for Doc to turn off the cameras, 'cause I'm gonna be all up in yo' vag." He stands up, pulling me with him, and leans over to clap Doc on the shoulder. "See ya tonight, bro."

Oh, fuck.

Seventeen

Seven

I HOLD TWYLA'S HAND AS WE walk to the end of the hallway, stopping at the door that opens to the staircase, which leads down to the club. She steps back, propping herself up against the wall next to my office, her eyes traveling up and down my body. The way she bites her lip tells me she likes what she sees— black boots, dark jeans, black Henley that fits over my muscles like a second skin. When her thorough inspection lands on the black leather hood in my hands, I see her swallow thickly.

I know she's nervous about tonight. But I also know that if I try to comfort her the way my instincts naturally want to, it makes her anxiety worse. I've learned it's better to pretend I don't see her worry and act like everything is fine, which it is. She responds better to my humor as a distraction to work through it, rather than focusing on what's bothering her. She feeds off my moods, so as long as I don't give in to my need to pull her against me and cradle her while I tell her everything's going to be all right, she'll relax and work through her inner conflict herself.

We've gotten to know each other so much over the last six weeks. It was in the two days she'd spent in the hospital after I carried her out of The Red Rocket I learned this quirk in her personality. And it was actually the monitor next to her bed that gave it away. Instinctively, I wanted to hold her, tell her I'd never let anything happen to her ever again, baby her, assure her I'd take a bullet for her, all while begging her forgiveness for allowing the fucker to get to her in the first place. Instead of all this providing her some sense of comfort, knowing she would forever be safe from that moment on, the monitors showed her blood pressure and pulse rising, all while her face was a mask of calm. So I stopped my groveling, and when I started forcing myself to make jokes and distract her as the nurses came in to change her bloody bandages, her blood pressure dropped and her pulse evened out.

I've heard of couples, mostly in D/s relationships, since that's who I'm around all the time, who are so in sync with each other that their moods are affected by how their partner is feeling. I had never experienced this before, always being able to ignore my once grumpy-ass best friend Corbin, or straight-faced and serious Bryan, or scholarly Doc, their personalities having no effect on my mostly shiny outlook. So now I tap into that when I suspect Twyla is feeling nervous or anxious, because I know she'll respond better if I let her feed off my jovialness instead of trying to soothe her.

I saunter up to her, my wicked grin in place as I cage her in with my arms against the wall. Her breath quickens, just like it always does when I look at her this way, making me feel powerful in a way I never felt before her. I have no idea if this expression would have an effect on any other woman because I've always worn my mask, but it doesn't matter. I save the look for Twyla alone, loving the way it makes her eyes go half-mast and her chest flush. She obviously loves feeling like my prey.

I lean down and nuzzle her neck then whisper in her ear, "Once I put this mask on, I'm not longer Seth. My little doll will submit to me as her Dom, and I'll take care of you in ways you never imagined. When we walk through that door, you'll refer to me as either Seven or Master, whichever one feels most natural to you. But no matter how differently I touch you or speak to you when we're in the playroom, no matter how hard I fuck you to the point you think I hate you, even as you beg for more, just know I love you with everything I am."

She shudders against me, whimpering, "Okay," as she grips my shirt over my stomach, her breasts rising and falling quickly as her body heat soaks into my front.

I step back, pulling the mask over my head. When the eyeholes and opening over my lips are in place, I meet her gaze, seeing my hood has the effect on her that it has on all the subs downstairs. It brings forth a slight amount of fear, being unable to see the emotions going on behind the mask. It makes one forget the usually friendly, smiling face when it's covered by such a dark, almost menacing hood. Gone are my playful expressions, my attractive features, and my approachable appearance, and in their place is something similar to an executioner's mask, one that makes people naturally want to look away, unable to meet my eyes behind it.

She glances downward, and that's when I pull a gift for her

out of my pocket. I'd asked her to wear contacts tonight instead of her glasses, just so they'd be out of the way for the pretty dark red lace mask I now hold in my hands for her to see.

"Oh, it's beautiful," she breathes, tracing her finger around the scalloped edge that would sit on her nose.

"A little welcome present for my doll. I can't tell you how happy I am to have you as a member of my club, lovely Twyla. There's nothing I want more than to share every aspect of my life with you," I tell her, and then place the delicate lace across her eyes, circling around the back of her hair to tie it into a knot to make sure it doesn't slip off during our scene. When I tilt her face up by her chin, her deep blue eyes sparkle, framed by the dark red mask as she smiles. "Fucking perfect," I growl, lifting my hood for just a moment to kiss her gently before putting it back in place. "You ready?"

At her nod, I take her hand once again before opening the door. The club's sensual thumping music fills our ears as we make our way down the stairs, and everyone in the main area, those on the dance floor, at the bar, and in the surrounding booths, turn their heads to watch our descent. Never before had they seen their trainer enter the club with someone. Everyone already knew I was now in a monogamous relationship. I had made that clear two months ago when I met Twyla and stopped participating in scenes with submissives. And they had all been waiting until this quarter's round of memberships to see if she would join us, and by the looks on all their faces, the small smiles and wide grins seen below their various masks, they're happy to finally get a glimpse of the woman who had stolen Seven's heart.

Those who were sitting climb to their feet, and everyone else squares their body to face us, and when we reach the bottom step and walk toward the crowd, they all bow their heads respectfully in welcome. Twyla shyly tucks herself against my side, but she smiles at everyone then up at me. I reach up and trace her exposed jawline, and she leans into my touch, turning her face to kiss the center of my palm.

At that, the club returns to life, members approaching to congratulate me on finding the sub I want to devote myself to, and Twyla on becoming a full-fledged member of Club Alias. Having been through the initiation themselves, they all know it's quite a feat.

Corbin and Vi appear in front of us, and she hands Twyla a glass of sparkling white wine, introducing herself. "Hi there. I'm... shit. I can't really say here, can I, Sir?" she asks, turning toward her husband.

He chuckles, shaking his head. "No, baby girl. But she knows who you are. Seven had her read your books."

I watch Twyla's face light up when she realizes who is standing before us. With Corbin wearing his signature black leather mask similar to mine and having never met Vi before, she hadn't recognized them until now.

"Oh my gosh," she gasps. "Excuse me while I fangirl. Your stories are freaking amazing."

"Aw, thank you. But it's only because I had your man to teach me about all the BDSM stuff," Vi tells her, her eyes twinkling up at me from beneath her black lace mask.

"Only the first series," Corbin complains. "It wasn't until you started learning hands-on that you wrote your best-selling stories yet, and that was all me."

Vi smiles at her husband. "How very right you are, Sir," she purrs.

"On that note," I insert, "I believe it's time I finally show my doll what the playrooms are really for. You two have a wonderful night."

"You too. So nice to finally meet you. And welcome to the family," Vi tells Twyla, who beams before I take her hand and lead her away.

"I like her," she whispers up to me, and then takes a sip of her wine. "What does she mean by family, though? Is that what everyone calls each other here at the club?"

I reach over and take the glass from her hand, and she pouts up at me.

"I want you sober for this, doll. It's important you have a perfectly clear head this first time, especially for such a delicate situation," I explain, setting the glass on a tray carried by a passing waitress as we head around the booths toward the third playroom on the left—the one that holds the two instruments I'll be using on her tonight. "And no. She means our little family. The guys and I are more like brothers, and I'm sure she is happy to finally have another woman to hang out with outside the club. She's normally the only one at get-togethers."

"That is pretty exciting. I've never really had a close girlfriend before. Just my sis—"

Her words cut off as we step into the playroom and I yank the curtain closed, reality settling in on what we're here to do. Her face instantly goes from animated to nervous, her anxiety returning now that she doesn't have anything distracting her. And unfortunately, when I'm in a playroom, my usual joking nature takes a back seat to the more serious, commanding yet sensual side of me. Sometimes it feels like I have a split personality, the way my two halves never seem to mix, especially compared to

Corbin, who's the way he is 100 percent of the time, whether he's at the club or not. I just pray Twyla will love Seven as much as she loves Seth.

I flip a switch on the wall, which will turn on a red light outside the door indicating the room is occupied and marked as private. No one will come inside to watch the scene taking place.

"And we begin," I state, drawing her attention from the devices I set out earlier in preparation for tonight. "Normally, I would have you strip down completely and place your clothes inside the trunk." I gesture toward the black footlocker next to the door. "But in this instance, since we do have an audience..." I point up at the security cameras in the corners of the room. "...I will let you decide how many items you feel comfortable removing. Just be aware in order to get the full effect of the instruments I'll be properly introducing you to, I will need a vast amount of your beautiful skin exposed," I tell her gently, being careful not to say anything about what happened to her. I only want good memories associated with my playroom, so I'll never speak of her attack while we're here.

Her mouth twists below her mask, a habit she has when making an important decision. A moment later, she walks over to the trunk and opens it, propping the lid against the wall. She starts with her black heels, slipping them off and placing them inside. Resting her hands on her neck, she turns her back to me and then peeks over her shoulder.

I step up to her, reaching for the tiny black zipper and sliding it down the hidden seam. I trace her spine with my fingertip, making her shiver, before stepping back again for her to continue.

She faces me once more, slipping the straps of her little black dress off her shoulders, letting it slide down her soft curves before stepping out of it. She folds it twice before putting it inside the trunk then stands up straight, looking absolutely fuckable in her black lace bra and matching panties. My cock swells to life taking in her incomparable beauty. And knowing I'm the only man who's ever touched her perfect body makes her striptease all the more sensual.

She reaches out and closes the lid on the footlocker, silently telling me that's as far as she's comfortable going while Doc watches behind the camera in his office.

"Very good, doll. Now, lie down on the padded table, on your back," I order, watching her put on a brave face as she follows my instructions.

Twyla

I LIE BACK on the black leather padded table and then turn my head to face Seven, watching him warily as he approaches. It's very easy to think of him as Seven and not Seth, because not only does his mask hide his handsome, smiling face, but his demeanor since entering the club has been completely different than the cheerful man I love. Yet something about his seriousness here is wildly erotic.

Picking up what I now know is a studded flogger, he reaches for my hand and places the tails in the center of my open palm. I fight the urge to yank it away as if he's setting a spider in my hand. Tamping down my fear, I feel the leather is surprisingly soft, completely opposite of what I had imagined by the way it had torn my skin open.

"Quality can make quite a difference, doll," he says softly, reading my thoughts. "This is genuine brushed leather with rounded stainless steel studs. There are cheaper versions, made of harsh, sharp-edged plastic, some with pointed studs. A tool like that should never be used on someone with such delicate skin."

He places my hand on the table next to my hip, and I brace myself as he swoops the flogger over my skin, still expecting the tails to be as painful as before. But my body immediately relaxes when I feel its gentle caress. Where the one I had experienced before was like razor blades, this one, as he begins a steady, swiping rhythm up and down my front, from my breasts down to the middle of my thighs then back up again, is more like the focused hands during a shiatsu massage.

"Turn onto your stomach," he orders, and I roll over. He picks his pattern back up again, working the studded flogger from the tops of my shoulders, down over my ass to the backs of my thighs, then back up again. And I can't help the moan that slips out as the hypnotic rhythm lulls me into a relaxed state I never thought I'd feel around the tools that'd hurt me so badly before.

Soon, heat pools between my legs as I fully give in to the sensations Seven provides with the leather tails, and I realize, slightly embarrassed, that my hips are instinctively moving against the padded table. I make an effort to stop, but Seven delivers a harder smack to my butt with the flogger, making me suck in a breath, but not out of pain.

"Never hide your pleasure from me, doll. The effort I put into giving you these feelings, making you let go of your inhibitions, is rewarded by your body taking over your mind. Just give in. Don't stop yourself from enjoying what you feel," he commands, and I melt into the table, doing exactly what he wants.

Before long, I'm a panting, groaning mess, my ass lifting into the air as he makes his way down my body with the flogger, hoping his masterful hand will somehow slip and accidentally stroke against my now throbbing pussy. It feels like if I don't have something touch me there soon, I'll burst from wanting.

But, of course, he doesn't miss, his aim perfectly accurate, landing across my lace-covered cheeks.

"Please!" I finally sob, and his sensual torture abruptly stops.

Suddenly, his black mask is level with my face as he leans down, and I can just barely make out the beautiful eyes I love so much deep in the shadows of the hood. "A sub does not ask her Dom for anything unless ordered to. You take the pleasure I give you unless I tell you to beg. Understand?" His voice is that demanding tone that goes straight to my pussy, and all I can do is nod. "I require verbal responses when I ask you a question in my playroom, doll."

"Yes, Master," I reply, remembering how I'm supposed to address him in the club.

He's so close I hear him swallow behind his hood, and if I'm not mistaken, his eyes close briefly, as if he's stopping to appreciate my show of respect. After a moment, he reaches up to gently brush my sweaty hair out of my face as he whispers, "Such a good girl." And I melt under his praise.

He sets down the flogger, and I feel his warm hand rest on my ankle before it slowly makes its way up my leg and between my thighs. His fingers press against my core, over my panties, and I hear his exhale of breath.

"My little doll is soaked," he says, his voice gruff. "Yet we have one more thing to explore before I give you relief."

I swallow my whimper, not wanting to complain and

disappoint him. He pulls over a rolling table with a wooden box on top.

"On your back," he demands, and with great effort, since my body feels like Jell-O, I roll over, facing up.

"This is a violet wand. It is not meant to sit still against your flesh but rather be moved across your skin to create a tingling sensation along its path. But before I begin, I need to explain something. This is just a demonstration for you to feel how these tools are meant to be used. If you decide you enjoy these things and want to do a full scene using them, we will establish safewords—words you can call during a scene to let me know you either don't like what's happening and want me to back off a little or if you want me to completely stop. But for now, this is just a taste. I only want you to sample what this device feels like," he explains, and it makes me feel better that he isn't going to force me to endure something if I absolutely hate it.

Not that I think Seven would ever make me do something I don't want. Even if this side of him is a lot different than my sweet Seth, he's still the same man I love, and who I know loves me just as much.

He turns the wand on, and a light hum fills my ears. "The farther away from the skin I hold the wand, the more intense the feeling. So I'll start close, and then gradually move away," he tells me, taking hold of my hand once again.

I force myself to breathe steadily as he holds the device close to my fingertip, but I gasp as the glowing blue light appears like a bolt of lightning forming a bridge between my flesh and the glass tube. Since my vision is clear this time, I see it almost looks like one of those Halloween decorations, the glass balls with the glowing lights inside that follow your fingertips as you slide them along the outside. Only the bolt of light actually touches your skin with the violet wand, feeling like static electricity zapping in a steady arc.

As he did with the flogger, he places my hand back on the table and then begins to glide the wand a couple inches away from my body, staying mostly below my waist. It tingles the flesh of my hips, down my legs, tickling the bottom of my feet, before moving back up my thighs. But much sooner than he did with the other toy, he sets it down. He must sense I'm now more comfortable with the tool, but it's doing nothing for me sexually.

"And that, my doll, is the proper way to use the violet wand. There are more attachments, more intensities, and settings, but mostly, that's the gist. You don't seem very impressed," he states.

"It was um... more annoying than anything," I admit, and I'm surprised to hear him chuckle.

"I agree. So now I'm going to introduce you to something else that is anything but annoying."

My eyes lift to him, and I watch as he makes a slicing motion across his throat toward one of the security cameras, and almost instantly, I see the tiny green light in each corner of the ceiling blink out.

"There's one more thing I need to show you the proper use for. Something that was used against you but is meant to help bring immeasurable amounts of pleasure. It involves trusting your Dom completely, and if you do, the reward is overwhelming," he says, walking over to the back wall to pull something off a hook. When he turns around, I tense when I see he's holding a set of shackles.

My immediate response is to get away, tears springing to my eyes, but I force myself to remain on the padded table as he approaches. My breath quickens, the salty droplets running from the corners of my eyes and into my hair as I face the ceiling. I'm surprised at how intense my reaction to seeing the shackles is, much more extreme than to the flogger and the violet wand. But then I recall how awful and terrifying it had been, unable to get away because of being bound to the table, being forced to endure the pain against my will.

My eyes squeeze shut as Seven comes to stand behind me at the head of the table, looking down at me from behind his leather hood. Every inch of me trembles, the relaxed state the flogger had put me in completely gone. I'm so tense that when Seven rests his hand on my shoulder in a caress meant to comfort, a gut-wrenching sob escapes me, causing my tears to come pouring out.

"Look at me, doll," Seven demands, but I shake my head, clamping my eyes shut tighter. "Twyla," he growls low, as not to let anyone hear my real name. Yet I still can't bring myself to look at him.

"I can't," I whimper, sniffling. "The mask. I can't do this with the mask. It could be him behind that hood. I can't. Please don't make me." My tears trickle to my ears, soaking my hairline.

I hear a swift movement above me, and then my love's deep, soothing voice. "It's gone, my beautiful doll. Look at me, sweet girl."

When I finally bring myself to open my lids, Seven's worried but mesmerizing hazel eyes fill my vision. I start to relax as I take in the softness of his gaze, his handsome, loving face framed by his light brown beard and thick eyebrows, looking nothing like the evil, dark man who had hurt me.

"He's in jail, Twyla," he whispers. "He'll be there till we're old and gray."

He leans down, kissing me upside-down, the hair on his chin tickling my nose. I breathe in his scent, the smell of his woodsy cologne mixed with leather soothing me as I open to him, his tongue dipping in to lick across mine. It feels sinfully delicious at this angle, the tops of our tongues slipping across each other making me moan. I reach up, my fingers sifting through his thick, short hair, and the familiar feeling allows the rest of my anxiety to slip away.

As he pulls back far enough to look into my eyes, he smiles down at me sweetly. "Remind me to put *Spiderman* on our list of movies to watch. Because damn, Toby and Kirsten were onto something with that upside-down kiss," he murmurs, and then he stands back up to his full height. I know he's breaking character just to calm my nerves, and it brings back the tranquility I had while in his masterful hands. When he sees I'm ready to continue with our scene, I watch, fascinated, as Seth steps back and Seven moves into place.

"Now, these are cuffs that attach to the table with a carabiner." He holds the black leather up for me to see, turning them over to show me the hardware. "They fasten with a buckle, not a lock and key like handcuffs or metal shackles. They're also padded and lined with soft felt, so they are much more comfortable around your arms. It will not hurt the delicate bones of your wrists if you pull against them."

This makes me feel much better, thinking back to the braces I had to wear on my wrists along with bandages for three weeks. I'd hurt myself pretty badly yanking against the metal shackles, and the doctor had said the violet wand's current had arced to the cuffs, giving me first-degree burns that were now fully healed a month and a half later. They told me I was lucky I was healthy, because it could have stopped my heart with the length of time he'd held the device straight to my ribs.

Seven loops one of the soft cuffs around my right wrist, pulling me back to the present as he tugs my arm above my head, fastening it to the padded table. He does the same to my left, and I give them a yank, feeling the cushioning around my wrists, but not a painful bite. I look up at him, giving him a single nod to let him know I'm okay.

"All right, doll. I want you to close your eyes and think back months ago to our first lesson. There was a toy I taught you about. One I offered you to take home to try out on your own, but you informed me you were a virgin," he says, his voice sending a thrill throughout my body as I remember that first day. I had been so nervous, yet so excited to spend time with the sexy stranger.

"The Wild Orchid," I reply on an exhale.

He circles the table, trailing his fingers down my body as he makes his way to the opposite end. "The Wild Orchid," he confirms, and a shiver runs through me when the sound of buzzing fills my ears, this one that of a vibrator instead of the electric crackling of the violet wand from earlier.

With my eyes still closed, I jump a little when he touches the toy to the inside of my calf, but then relax as he trails it upward, over my knee, before drawing little patterns along my inner thighs, teasing me with the vibrations until my legs instinctively fall open.

"Breathe, doll." His voice enters my consciousness, making me realize I was holding my breath in anticipation of his next move. When I empty my lungs and fill them with fresh oxygen, he skims the vibrator over my lace-covered center, sending me into a full body shudder as my knees try to close.

"Still," he commands, and I force my thighs to part, giving in to the overwhelming sensations at my core. My hips rotate of their own accord as I try to remember to breathe, my body feeling flushed as he presses the toy to my clit. I moan, unconsciously pulling at the cuffs around my wrists. He's playing with me, not giving me enough to get off, but making me needy with desire.

Suddenly, the vibrator vanishes from between my legs, and I whimper in disappointment until I feel him tugging my panties off. He takes hold of my thighs and yanks me toward the foot of the table, my arms stretching out straight above my head as my hands stay locked in place.

"Fuck me, your pretty pussy is soaked, little doll," he says, sounding feral as his fingers stroke over my swollen flesh. I can feel my pulse in my clit I'm so turned on, and I cry out as, all of a sudden, I feel his hot mouth cover me. He growls as he buries his face against me, sucking, licking, and nibbling at my pussy like he's ravenous.

When he pulls away, I don't have time to make a sound of complaint as he replaces his mouth with the tip of the toy at my entrance, and as he slowly sinks it inside me, the pointed tip widening into its bulbous shaft fills me, the vibrations against my inner walls making me see colors behind my closed lids until it's all the way in. And that's when he shifts his hold on the Wild Orchid, allowing the second, shorter shaft to come down on top of my clit.

My body tries to fold in on itself, but with my hands shackled and Seven's grip on my thigh as he holds the toy inside me with his other hand, I'm only able to arch my back, which only makes the vibrator sink deeper as the exterior one nestles between my folds.

"Oh, *fuck!*" I groan. I've never felt anything like it before. Even my massaging shower head has nothing on the mind-numbing power of the toy Seven wields like he created it himself. I can't see exactly what he's doing, but somehow he repositions the Wild Orchid inside me, tilting it in such a way that it hits exactly the right spot, and before I can even pull in my next breath, I scream as an orgasm takes over my entire body.

The vibrator turns off, and I shudder as he removes it. And while I float on a cloud of euphoria, I barely comprehend the fact Seven is unbuttoning and unzipping his jeans until he takes hold of my thighs before sinking himself into me all the way to the hilt. His entrance is easy with the amount of wetness I feel as he pulls back then thrusts deep. He sets a punishing pace as I grip the cuffs at the bottom of my hands, and with my pussy so sensitive from using the toy only minutes ago, before long, I'm calling out Seven's name as I come in a flood of body-wracking jolts.

But he doesn't stop to let me come down from the orgasm. Instead, he thrusts harder, deeper, growing rougher with each plunge, and I can't get enough. I open my eyes to look at my dark lover, his face twisted in concentration and pleasure. His thick eyebrows are pulled together over his eyes that are almost black with passion as he watches himself disappear into my blistering depths. His full lips are parted as he breathes deeply with each pump of his massive cock.

The sight of his strong fingers digging into my soft thighs does something to me, making my pussy clench around him, and he looks up my body and into my eyes. And with our gazes locked and one... two... three more violent thrusts, I come with a silent scream, my voice completely gone as if the pleasure itself has stolen it away, as he empties himself inside me.

He falls forward, collapsing on top of me, panting, his breath tickling my nipple where his head rests on my breasts. My thighs tremble around his hips, and I straighten out my legs, trying to get more comfortable. I want to wrap my arms around him, but am unable to because my wrists are still bound, making me wiggle in annoyance. He lifts his head to look at my face, and reads my thoughts as I tug at my hands.

He gives me a gentle smile, no words needing to be spoken as he reaches up and unbuckles the leather cuffs. My arms feel heavy as I bring them down to rest around his shoulders, and he nuzzles his face back between my breasts with a satisfied sigh.

I don't know how long we stay there, him resting inside me as our breathing evens out, but when he finally speaks, a smile spreads across my face.

"Welcome to the club, doll."

I clench around his thickness. "Thank you, Master."

Epilogue

Twyla

Seven years later

"**M**OMMY! COME WATCH OUR SHOW with us!" Luna calls from the living room as soon as I get home from work, where she's cuddled up to Seth eating popcorn.

"Yeah, Mommy. Come see," he urges, giving me his wicked grin over the top of our daughter's head.

My eyes narrow suspiciously, but I set down my purse, kick off my shoes, and go plop down on the couch with our girl between us. Seth's arm comes down around my shoulders across the back of the couch, and I relax, focusing in on the cartoon as I reach for a handful of popcorn.

"Look, Mommy! There's you!" Luna chirps, and my brow

furrows as she points to the weird-looking girl on the screen. The character has long teal and purple hair and lavender skin, so I'm not sure what she means. "And there's me!" she adds, bouncing on her bottom excitedly. This character has black and red pigtails with goldish-green skin.

"Okay," I drawl, glancing over at Seth, who has his lips pulled in between his teeth, fighting back laughter.

But then I hear it.

"Are you going to the party at Frankie's place, Luna?" the lavender girl says, and I look down at my daughter with surprise as she raises her perfect little face to see my reaction at hearing her name. Her beautiful hazel eyes, just like her daddy's, sparkle up at me with glee.

Turning my attention back to the TV, I see a different character, who looks oddly like a living gargoyle, return the question to the lavender girl. *"What about you, Twyla? You going to be there?"*

I gasp as my eyes shoot to Luna then Seth then back again. "No way! I've never heard of any character having my name before. That's super cool," I tell her, and she claps her little hands and giggles. The show goes to commercial, and the characters reappear on the screen, this time in an ad. My eyes narrow once again as the name comes from the TV. "Monster High Dolls?"

"Yeah, Mommy. They're the ones I asked for for my birthday, but you told me they sounded too scary," she says matter-of-factly, pooching her lips.

I ignore her jab and look over her head at Seth, who's turning red from holding back his laughter. "A character named Twyla.... Monster High *Dolls?*" I stress the last word, staring at my husband. "How long has this show been on, honey? Like, how many years?"

Luna switches the TV to Netflix, and in a matter of a few pushed buttons, she pulls up *Monster High*. "Started in 2010," comes her sweet voice, before she stuffs her mouth with popcorn and switches the TV back to her show.

"Are you telling me you got my nickname from a children's cartoon?" I whisper-yell at Seth, and then it hits me. "Which means you, a grown man, had been watching said children's cartoon... frequently enough to recall there was a character with my name?" My eyes grow wide as he throws his head back and laughs.

"Oh, come on, doll. This show is badass!" he proclaims.

Luna turns and wiggles her finger in front of his face. "You owe a dollar to the swear jar, Daddy! Only a few more dollars and we'll have enough for a trip to Wizarding World! Don't forget you promised."

He nods absently at her, used to being scolded for his bad language. "Seriously, Twy. The show is awesome. It's the children of all the classic monsters—the daughter of Frankenstein's monster, Dracula's little girl, the son of the river monster—and they all go to high school together."

I stare at him for a moment, and then my jaw drops. "Is this why you were so adamant on naming our child Luna?" He gives me a sheepish look, and I've got my answer. "You told me it was because you wanted to keep all the girl names in my family similar, all dealing with astrology." I drop my voice to mimic him. "'Yeah, doll. How cool would that be? Your name comes from the French word meaning 'star,' and your sis's name, Astrid, means 'Old Norse star.' Luna means 'moon,' so it would be like y'all are the moon and stars.'"

Over and over again, I had meant to Google the name

"Twyla" with "doll" to see why he always called me that, but then I would forget. After a while, I had just grown used to it, and never looked it up. All these years later, I'm just now learning my badass mercenary, Dominant, BDSM club owning, genius husband, who had once nearly strangled a man to death in front of me while rescuing me from being kidnapped, used to watch children's cartoons... before we had children.

The thought is utterly ridiculous, and I toss my head back and laugh until tears stream down my cheeks.

"Shh, Mommy!" Luna hisses at me when I look at the screen and see her show is back on.

I kiss the top of her head and pull her against my chest, leaning close to Seth and glaring as I whisper, "You're about to be killed by a Zamboni."

He bites his lip, reaching over to cover Luna's ears. "God, you know it makes me hard when you quote *Deadpool* to me, doll." Our daughter tries to wiggle out of his grip, but he holds steady as he gives me another one of his wicked grins. "Now, how about you meet me in the bedroom in five? Daddy needs to express some rage."

I giggle as he quotes our favorite movie. We can go back and forth all day, speaking to each other in nothing but lines from *Deadpool*, to the annoyance of all our friends. I give him a nod and stand up from the couch as he lets go of Luna's head. I circle around the back and lean over him.

I kiss his cheek then flick his ear with my tongue, ready to meet him in our room. But not before whispering, "Sounds good, because you've got a face I'd be happy to sit on."

The End

Please take a moment to leave a short review.
Every single one is greatly appreciated!

Join my reader group on Facebook!
KD-Rob's Mob
https://www.facebook.com/groups/KDRobsMob/

Acknowledgements

Let's see if I can keep this short and sweet this time, shall we? *giggles Yeah, right.

First, thank you, JJ Cadwell. You inspired an entirely brand new voice inside my head, one that became the comedic relief in Corbin and Vi's dark tale (Confession Duet). When I polled my Mobsters—my amazing reader group—asking whose book they wanted to read next, Seth was the winner hands down. And I was all too happy to oblige, because it would take me back to what I love writing, something with a more humorous touch like No Trespassing. Seth's mannerisms, his goofiness, his sweet nature and heart of gold, all came from you, so thank you for being such a great muse. Also, thank you for my incredible cover photo. My only instruction was "Look like the smiling devil face emoji" and you nailed it. I get chills every time I look at it. Oh! BTW, that is the "wicked grin" Seth always gives Twyla in the story, in case anyone was wondering. And thank you, Golden Czermak, for editing JJ's photo for me. I will forever be a Golden Girl!

To my badass besties, Bec, Laura, and Sierra. Without y'all to brainstorm out loud with, this story wouldn't have happened.

Thank you for letting me bounce my squirrel moments off of you until they miraculously start to line up and make a story. And my awesome beta girls, Stacia and Crystal, you always give me the confidence I need to keep at this writing gig.

My marvelous Hot Tree babes—Becky (my head honcho), Barb, and Mandy—I'm so proud to have y'all edit my books. Along with Cassy Roop of Pink Ink Designs, who creates covers and interiors that are like an orgasm for your eyeballs, you guys are my freaking dream team. I truly love you girls so much and don't know what I'd do without y'all.

I got to spend an entire month with my Aussie bestie, Bec, keeping her hostage in Texas and not letting her go home for two weeks longer than she originally planned. At some point during her captivity, she pointed out that *Seven* would be my seventh novel. And jokingly, I said, "Wouldn't it be cool to release *Seven*, my seventh book, on 7/7/17?" I had scoffed, looking at the date and seeing I would only have a month to write this bad boy, get it edited, and then send it to Cassy for formatting. But with Bec's simple, "Fucking do it," and with Jeananna's "I'm putting you down for that date," I made it a goal and, as you can see, I freaking did it! Thank you, Bec, for believing in me and pushing me like you knew for a fact I wouldn't fail. And thanks, Jeananna Banana, for your contagious enthusiasm. You and Kylie at Give Me Books really know how to take all the stress of a book release away.

Red Phoenix, you are my all-time favorite BDSM author. For years now, I have been spreading the word about Brie, and now it is such an honor to include something of yours in one of my own books.

Readers, in case you've been hiding under a rock, or maybe you have her on your TBR and keep getting distracted by other books, Red Phoenix is fucking BRILLIANT and you need to read her NOW. Seth studied BDSM under Master Anderson at The Academy in Denver. This is an homage to one of my favorite Doms in Red's Brie series. Seven was whispering to me that he was one of his students, and with Red's permission, she let me include that little tidbit of Seth's past in my story.

So thank you, Red, for just being you. The author became the muse. <3

Finally, thank you to my hubbyface, Jason, for letting me work at all hours. I know this is a challenge for you, you needy motherfucker, always wanting to cuddle and shit. I love you and our girls more than Reese's. And you know how much I love Reese's.

<3